"I wish Ms. Kelsey could be my new mommy."

Those nine words from Mia made Zach question his parenting and his decision to remain single, and left him with his heart hammering in his chest. That's what he got for listening in on their conversation.

Zach had placed the basket down and was now waiting for Morgan's answer. He had to remain quiet so he could hear her much-softer tone.

"But she's already my auntie" came the quiet reply.

He placed a hand over his mouth to cover his chuckle. He wished he had brought his phone with him to record this conversation. Kelsey would have enjoyed hearing Morgan speak at least five words.

"I know, but if she married my daddy, then we would be together."

On second thought, perhaps it was a good thing he wasn't recording this. He didn't know how Kelsey would react.

"I want us to be together," Morgan breathed out.

"Then tell Ms. Kelsey to marry Daddy," Mia said. Then she used one of Zach's expressions. "It's that simple."

Zoey Marie Jackson loves writing sweet romances. She is almost never without a book and reads across genres. Originally from Jamaica, West Indies, she has earned degrees from New York University; State University of New York at Stony Brook; Teachers College, Columbia University; and Argosy University. She's been an educator for over twenty years. Zoey loves interacting with her readers. You can connect with her at zoeymariejackson.com.

Books by Zoey Marie Jackson

Love Inspired

The Adoption Surprise

Visit the Author Profile page at LoveInspired.com.

The Adoption Surprise

Zoey Marie Jackson

LOVE INSPIRED
INSPIRATIONAL ROMANCE

LOVE INSPIRED®

INSPIRATIONAL ROMANCE

Recycling programs
for this product may
not exist in your area.

ISBN-13: 978-1-335-56759-8

The Adoption Surprise

This edition published by arrangement with Harlequin Books S.A.

For questions and comments about the quality of this book, please contact us
at CustomerService@Harlequin.com.

Love Inspired
22 Adelaide St. West, 41st Floor
Toronto, Ontario M5H 4E3, Canada
www.LoveInspired.com

Printed in U.S.A.

For God hath not given us the spirit of fear;
but of power, and of love, and of a sound mind.
—*2 Timothy* 1:7

For my darling, John, a man of faith and the one God used to help me believe in love again. Thank you for all the talk throughs with the characters and story lines.

I also would like to acknowledge my sons, Eric and Jordan, my stepchildren and my family, who are my biggest motivators and supporters. I also have to mention my *Sisters* writing group and my critique partner, Vanessa Miller, as well as my sister, Sobi Burbano, for her feedback.

Special thanks to my editor, Dina Davis, and my agent, Latoya Smith. I feel blessed to have been given the opportunity to write for this line.

Chapter One

For the third time that Thursday morning, Kelsey Harris fought back tears. And for the hundredth time over the past six months, she questioned her ability to be a mother.

Her niece, Morgan, had been given the world's most amazing parents for almost six years. Then in a moment, at the hands of a reckless drunk driver, both her parents had been snatched away in a nasty collision with Morgan in the back seat.

Now all she had was Kelsey.

An inadequate substitute.

She stood in the kitchen of her sister's house—her house now—in the small community of Swallow's Creek, Delaware, ignoring the empty Chinese food containers mixed in with the clutter on the kitchen counter and the stack of dishes in the sink. Instead, Kelsey watched

Morgan swing her legs under the small round kitchen table, eating her Lucky Charms slower than the first pour of ketchup from a bottle. Kelsey didn't dare rush her for fear that Morgan would stop eating.

The child already barely ate.

Or spoke.

Her vibrant, fun-loving five-year-old niece had been replaced with one enclosed in a silent cocoon. Kelsey didn't know how to get Morgan back to herself.

Reason number 4,673 why Kelsey doubted her skills. Oh, why had God put her in this position?

Morgan took another spoonful—her fourth—her hand moving from bowl to mouth, lackluster. A chore.

Sitting down in a chair across from Morgan, Kelsey braced herself to ask a question that made her heart pound. "I heard you crying last night. But when I came in the room, you turned away from me. I know you were awake and pretending to be asleep. Do you want to talk about it?"

Her niece closed her eyes and shook her head.

"Sweetie, you can talk to me about anything regarding your mom and dad. And how you feel. I want to help you."

Kelsey tensed while she prayed and begged

God to loosen her niece's tongue. All she got was another shake of the head. She didn't push for fear Morgan would become upset and stop eating.

Patting Morgan's hand, she said, "Okay, honey. Finish your breakfast."

After a brief hesitation, Morgan squared her shoulders and resumed eating. Kelsey released a plume of air.

Maybe it was good she had finally heeded Pastor Reid's advice. He had recommended a Christian therapist, Lily Hernandez, who was trained in childhood trauma. After months of lagging, Kelsey had made the appointment for the following Thursday, June 23. It was an hour away in Wilmington, but Morgan's well-being was worth the drive. Kelsey had plugged the details into her calendar and set an alarm reminder to make sure she didn't forget. If therapy didn't work, Kelsey was seriously considering a move to San Diego or Florida. Both she and Morgan could use a little sunshine in their lives.

Kelsey looked at the clock and bit back a groan. She had thirty minutes until the meeting with her new client, but she had to drop Morgan off at the first day of summer camp. As one of the top real estate agents in Swallow's Creek, Kelsey stayed busy and worked past midnight most days. But once she became Morgan's primary caretaker, she'd had to reduce her hours. One of the perks of being in business for herself in a small town was that she could do the daily drop-off and pickup from school. Not bad for a twenty-nine-year-old cosmetology school dropout.

Which in itself was a plus. Morgan's hair was always on point. Kelsey eyed her niece's shoulder-length cornrows and beads with pride. Morgan's hair shone, moving and swaying while Morgan chewed her food. Slowly.

Seconds later, Morgan plopped her spoon in the bowl and stood, causing the chair to scrape across the floor.

"Are you all done, honey?" Kelsey asked, swallowing the disappointment when she saw how much was left.

With a nod, Morgan picked up her bowl, holding it close to her chest. Kelsey knew Morgan was afraid it might fall and shatter to pieces like two others had before. Yet, if she offered to help, Morgan would refuse. Her niece placed the bowl in an empty spot on the counter, then tugged her Moana T-shirt over her brown leggings. She had outgrown the outfit but refused to allow Kelsey to change out her wardrobe. Their last trip to the mall had been a disaster, with Morgan crying and asking for her mom.

"Can you use your words for Auntie?" Kelsey pleaded, tucking Morgan under the chin.

Her niece looked up at her with sad, haunted eyes, her jaw churning behind zipped lips. A few seconds passed before she whispered, "Yes."

"Great," Kelsey said with a cheer she didn't feel. She gave Morgan a quick hug. "Why don't you get your Princess Tiana bag?" With a nod, Morgan went to get her backpack. It was one of the last things Kennedy had purchased for Morgan, and it was her niece's prized possession. Morgan didn't go anywhere without it, though it was almost as big as she was.

Once they were out the door, Kelsey swallowed the muggy heat, rushed to her BMW coupe and directed Morgan to get in her booster chair and put on her seat belt. She really needed to trade this car in and get a sensible mom car.

And she would. Probably never.

She couldn't bear to part with her car.

Kelsey put on JoJo Siwa, then glanced in her mirror to see if Morgan danced along. But the former ballerina sat still, eyes wide as she clutched the leather seats. Kelsey wanted to tell her niece not to worry, but she, too, had been traumatized. The first week after Kennedy's and Alex's deaths, Kelsey had been too paranoid to drive. One of her best friends, Sienna

King, had done the driving. Kelsey had had to recite 2 Timothy 1:7 several times before she got behind the wheel again.

She was halfway to the summer camp when she slapped her forehead. "I forgot to pack your lunch." She rebuked her self-recriminating thoughts.

Morgan shrugged and peered out the window.

"I'll get you a burger and fries for lunch. How's that sound?"

Her niece nodded. Kelsey couldn't imagine the horror Morgan relived every time they got inside a vehicle. Her heart squeezed tight, like a lollipop in a child's fist. She wished she could snap her fingers and remove the pain that Morgan must be feeling. Or take that agony onto herself.

Sinking into her seat, Kelsey whispered an internal prayer. *Please, God. Help me help her. 'Cause I don't have a clue.*

By this time, Kelsey had twelve minutes to meet her client. She gripped the wheel and resisted the urge to press down on the accelerator. That might scare Morgan. She would prefer to be late and lose that deal rather than cause Morgan any additional harm. So she counted to ten and followed the speed limit.

Kelsey pulled into the church parking lot and drove to the rear, toward the camp entrance.

There was a huge black SUV in the lane. Just as she moved to turn, the rear door of the truck opened and a pink ball bounced in front of her car. A small girl jumped out and went after the ball. All Kelsey saw was a head full of curls as she squealed with horror.

Panicked, Kelsey stomped on her brakes. The tires screeched like squawking seagulls as the car hurtled forward. Morgan emitted an earsplitting scream. And then another. Kelsey rammed the gear into Park, jabbed the release button on her seat belt and grabbed Morgan's leg to comfort her. Morgan's eyes were shut tight, her face red, her horror evident.

A tall, muscular man dressed in a pair of gray slacks and a blue-and-white-checkered shirt came after the child and scooped her into his arms.

Stealing a quick glance and seeing the other little girl had not been hurt, Kelsey yelled, "It's all right, Morgan," before opening her door with such force it rocked on the hinges. She catapulted out of the vehicle and scuttled to the passenger side to open Morgan's door.

With sweaty hands, Kelsey fumbled before undoing Morgan's seat belt. Morgan lunged toward Kelsey, her little body shaking and her chest heaving. Kelsey scooped the quivering child into her arms and rocked her, kissing the top of her head. "It's okay. It's okay. You're fine, Morgan. You're fine." Morgan bellowed directly in her ear. She tilted her head, her ear cavity ringing. Her niece had quite the healthy pair of lungs.

Feeling a presence looming behind her, Kelsey turned. She was tall, at five-ten, but she had to look up at the man. And her eyes enjoyed the journey, taking in his full lips and square jaw and stopping in awe at a pair of unusual eyes—one hazel, the other a deep, rich honey brown. She swallowed, having never met anyone with heterochromia before, and tried to hide her instant fascination.

She lowered her eyes, resisting the urge to fan herself. Did he notice how flustered she was? The stranger hadn't said a word. That was odd. She scrunched her nose and made her eyes meet his.

His gaze was trained on… *Morgan?* Kelsey frowned, snapping out of her musings and swallowing her awakened fury. You'd think he would be apologizing or thanking her, but instead he stood staring at Morgan, like he was judging her niece for screaming and crying. His daughter slid down his body to hide behind his leg.

Kelsey swung around to shield Morgan from the man's intense gaze.

"I'm glad your daughter is okay," she said,

raising a brow. Her tone had enough acid to so-
licit a reaction.

The man sputtered like a choked engine. "I'm
sorry. I'm glad you saw Mia jump out of my
truck. If you hadn't…"

"The main thing is that I did see her and that
she's safe." Kelsey tried to put Morgan down,
but her niece clung to her tighter than a mon-
key on a swing. Morgan had stopped screaming and had wiped her face into Kelsey's blouse.
Her sniffles tore at Kelsey's heart.

"Are you okay?" she asked, noting that the
man was still, as if he was in shock.

He stepped back, rubbing his eyes. "Nope.
My eyes aren't deceiving me. I am seeing doubles." He tried to tug the little girl from his leg,
but she was holding on to him.

"Doubles? Really?" Kelsey asked, moving
away from him. She didn't have time for corny
pickup lines or to engage with someone more
concerned with hitting on a woman than tending
to his child. She retrieved Morgan's book bag,
then swung her hips to close the car door. With
long strides, she went to the driver's side to shut
that door as well. Kelsey tried not to think of
her damp blouse and her bun coming undone.

"Wait," the man said, but she lifted her chin
and kept moving. She thought she heard the
sound of an alarm behind her. This man defi-

nitely wasn't from around here. Hardly anybody in Swallow's Creek locked their vehicles.

Zachary Johnson watched the woman scurrying up the path, struggling to keep her rapid pace with a child in her arms. A child that, if his eyes were seeing right, was the mirror image of his daughter, Mia.

A doppelgänger.

His heart thumped in his chest, and goose bumps popped up on his arms. It couldn't be. Zach needed to get another glimpse. Then he could laugh at his error and apologize for freaking out her mother. He hadn't had much sleep the past few nights, having just relocated to Swallow's Creek from Philadelphia.

"Why was that girl screaming, Daddy?" Mia asked, peering around his leg and looking up at him. "I'm scary." Her chin wobbled, melting his heart. His little pumpkin, as he called her, had him wrapped about her finger. Fortunately, she didn't know it.

"You mean scared." Zach patted her curls and corrected her. "I don't know, honey. Maybe she was afraid."

The fact that Mia could have been hit by a vehicle registered. Not even five minutes ago, Zach could have lost his baby girl. An image of her lifeless body flashed before him and his legs weakened. He snatched Mia in his arms again and hugged her tight. She squirmed, her back arching like mozzarella cheese against him, but Zach couldn't let her go. His baby was alive and well.

Unlike Sandy. His wife had passed after losing a battle with cancer two years ago. They had gotten married at twenty-one, and he treasured the eleven years they'd had together. Sandy had truly been his best friend.

"Put me down, Daddy," Mia said, pulling on his goatee. "I'm not a baby. I'm a big girl. I can walk."

"You'll always be my baby," Zach said, willing his legs to move.

Then he stopped. With all the commotion, he had forgotten Mia's lunch box. He put Mia down and kept his eyes on her as he ran to retrieve her pink ball. Her ruffled pink skirt looked like it had snagged, and the T-shirt was no longer tucked in. Most of her hair had come undone from her lopsided ponytail. It had taken him fifteen minutes to undo her tangles and get it in a ponytail.

Zach hated to see her so disheveled, especially on her first day of summer camp. But he had to get back to the house. There was a truck coming to deliver Sandy's car, and he had to be there to open the garage.

Thankfully, his chatty new neighbor, Jade Wilson, had shown up a couple days ago with a scrumptious walnut cake in her hand to welcome him to the neighborhood. When he mentioned Mia, who had been asleep upstairs, she had suggested Millennial House of Praise's summer camp. Jade had left after that, promising to come by soon with her fifteen-year-old daughter, Izabelle, whom she had volunteered for babysitting if he needed it.

"Hurry up, Daddy," Mia said, flapping her arms like a baby bird trying out its wings. "I'm ready to go."

Zach returned to his truck, tossed the ball in the back and stretched across the seat for Mia's lunch box. Taking her hand in his, he started back up the path to the entrance of the camp. Mia danced and twirled the entire way.

"I'm going to make twenty new friends," Mia said.

He chuckled. "Twenty? That's a lot of friends. You only need one or two."

"I still want twenty." She skipped.

As soon as he walked through the door, warmth akin to the first bite of fluffy pancakes seeped through him. The walls were painted with images of Noah's ark, David and Goliath, and other biblical heroes. There were about thirty children ranging in age from four to twelve scattered throughout the huge room. The young children herded together, their bodies moving like marionettes to the Chicken Dance. Some of the older children were sprawled in chairs in front of a large television screen, the rumble of T. D. Jakes's voice a low hum. Others busied themselves on their cell phones or on computers. His eyes scanned the play-kitchen area, theater tent and a mini racetrack—an organized chaos.

Zach counted six counselors milling about the room, recognizable by their blue T-shirts with Millennial House of Praise Camp Counselor emblazoned across the chest in white. He approached one and asked for Sienna King. While the teen scurried to get her, he appreciated the aroma of cinnamon rolls. He could almost taste the icing, picturing it oozing on the sides. His stomach growled. He hadn't had time for his protein shake that morning.

Mia loosened out of his grip to run over to where some girls stood playing with dolls. He searched for the little girl that looked like his daughter, but neither she nor her mother were in sight. If it weren't for his legs, which still felt like caving, Zach would have thought he was in a weird dream.

Then their absence was explained when he saw them come out of an office with another lady, whom he assumed was Sienna King, since she approached him with a hand outstretched. She was plus-size with a wide smile and deep dimples.

"Hello, you must be Zachary Johnson." Her voice was bubbly and light.

He nodded. "Yes, we spoke over the phone. Thanks for allowing me to drop my daughter off and register her the same day."

"Oh, it's not a problem. I'm glad you called when you did, because we're almost at capacity. Here is the paperwork for you to sign, and you have to complete the emergency contact information."

"Thank you so much," he said, taking the documents she offered. He noticed the other woman still clutched the little girl in her arms and seemed to be trying to get her to stay. He strained to focus on Sienna's words, but his attention was on the little girl. He couldn't see her face, but he knew that body, that frame, that hair. He knew it well.

"Mr. Johnson?"

He shook his head. "I'm sorry. I…" He pointed to where the woman stood. "Who is that?"

Sienna whipped her head to follow his finger. "That's my best friend, Kelsey." She gave him a suggestive smile. "She's single, if that's what you're asking."

He took a step back and held up a hand. "No, I'm not talking about her. I mean, who's the little girl with her? She looks just like—"

The woman lost her smile. "Like who?" she asked with a drawl in her tone that suggested she was ready to get on the defensive.

He knew he must look dumbstruck, but Zach's mind couldn't process what he was seeing.

Zach rushed to explain. "Let me introduce you to my daughter. I think when you see her, you'll understand." He called out to Mia, and when his daughter ran over, Sienna's eyes widened.

She sputtered. "This is your daughter?"

"Her name is Mia."

"That can't be," she said, shaking her head. "This is Morgan."

He splayed his hands. "Exactly."

Sienna's mouth hung open. "Oh, my." She swung around and shouted, "Kelsey. Come over here. You've got to see this."

The woman approached, and Zach's breath caught. His mind had been so occupied with the child in her arms that he hadn't seen her mother. But he was seeing her now. For sure. From her bronze-colored skin to her pouty lips and the purposeful sway in her stride, this woman emitted confidence.

Kelsey. The name suited her.

Zach looked away to compose himself. He had no right noticing her radiant beauty. He swallowed. Now that he had seen her, there was no unseeing her.

When she spotted Mia and he heard her harsh intake of breath, he said, "Our daughters have an uncanny resemblance."

"There's nothing uncanny about it," Sienna chimed in. "You can tell they are twins just by looking at them."

Twins. His insides twisted. No, it couldn't be.

Kelsey lifted a hand to her mouth. "How? How? They are like carbon copies."

A squeal and a scream quieted the entire room. The girls had discovered each other and had polar opposite reactions.

"She looks like me," Mia said, clapping her hands. The other little girl wasn't as delighted. In fact, to Zach, there was only one way to describe her face.

Terrified.

Chapter Two

Shivering, Morgan pulled on Kelsey's blouse before pointing at the other little girl. There was genuine fear in her eyes.

Kelsey willed her own rapidly beating heart to slow down as she looked Morgan in the eyes and said, "It's okay. Don't be alarmed, honey. We'll figure this out."

"She looks like me," Morgan whispered.

"I know" was all Kelsey could say. She was too busy trying not to show her excitement at those four spoken words.

Four amazing words that made Kelsey want to give a shout of praise. Her niece had spoken a sentence. But she knew Morgan was frightened. So was she. Questions raced through her mind, and she struggled to think. Now she understood the man's reaction earlier.

By this time, all the children had crowded

around the room and stood with awed expressions on their faces. Sienna ushered the four of them into her office for some privacy, and Kelsey set Morgan on the ground.

"My name's Zach." The man offered her his free hand, camp papers clutched in his other.

Kelsey blinked, trying not to appear fascinated by his heterochromia, and held out a hand. "I'm Kelsey." When their hands connected, she drew in a breath.

He had a firm grip and a sturdy handshake. Plus, he was looking her in the eyes. Finally. Her father always said that was a sign a man had character. Well, if that was true, Zach had plenty of character and some to spare.

Sienna left them on their own to go see about getting the camp started, her long box braids swaying behind her. Kelsey tuned in to the girls while Zach wandered the room, looking at the camp pictures Sienna had on display.

"I'm Mia," Morgan's look-alike said, reaching for Morgan's arm.

Kelsey could feel Morgan tense beside her, but her niece didn't pull her arm away. Which was a good sign. Morgan's eyes were wide and fixed on Mia.

"What's your name?" Mia said.

"Morgan," her niece whispered.

Zach returned, standing a few feet away, observing their interaction. He kept looking at both girls, shaking his head like he couldn't process what was transpiring right before him.

"Both our names start with *M*," Mia said, giggling and clapping her hands. She pressed her lips together to make the *M* sound. Her eyes brightened with glee. "Ooh, look. Let's go play together. We're going to be best friends."

She tugged Morgan to the corner of the room, where there was an assortment of toys and books. Mia began asking a lot of questions, and Kelsey strained her ear to hear Morgan's replies. Morgan spoke too softly for Kelsey to understand what she was saying.

But her mouth was moving.

She was talking. Having a conversation.

Like normal.

In six minutes, Mia had accomplished what Kelsey hadn't been able to do in six months. Kelsey sniffled and dabbed at her eyes with the back of her index finger. She remembered her prayer that morning and felt awe at how God appeared to be answering her. She just hadn't seen His answer coming in the form of a look-alike.

It was all too much.

Glancing at the clock, she could see it was close to 9:00 a.m. It was a good thing she had already called her client to reschedule for later that afternoon. She plopped into one of the two armchairs to watch the girls.

"Mind if I sit here?" a deep baritone asked.

Kelsey jumped. She had been so enthralled with the girls, she had almost forgotten she wasn't the only adult in the room. Almost. There was no missing the tall, imposing man who smelled of…baby powder? Kelsey, who had been told she had a silver tongue, sat there in awkward silence, her words stuck in her throat, before giving a slight nod.

Zach scooted the other armchair close to her and grinned, showing off a set of beautiful white teeth her dentist mother would have appreciated.

"So, I'm going to tackle the elephant in the room and ask if your daughter is adopted, and if so, does she know?"

Kelsey nodded, grateful he had broached the topic uppermost in both their minds. "Morgan's actually my niece." She wiped a hand on her pants, ignoring the curiosity in his eyes. "But yes, she's adopted, and yes, she knows. Thankfully, my sister had the foresight to explain it to her, because this would have been too much for me to handle."

He put a hand to his chin and narrowed his eyes.

"So, I'm assuming your daughter is adopted

as well?" She posed her statement as a question in a gentle tone.

Zach nodded, shifting his focus to somewhere across the room. "Yes, she is. Sandy—" He waved a hand. "That's my, uh, wife. She was a breast cancer survivor and had been advised to wait to have children. But she wanted to be a mother so badly that we looked into adoption. We did some inquiries and were ecstatic to learn there was a newborn baby girl available. We jumped at the chance to welcome Mia into our lives."

He had a wife. Kelsey squelched her sudden disappointment and bit her lower lip to keep from asking about his wife's whereabouts.

Zach's openness gave Kelsey the courage to share. "My sister, Kennedy, and her husband, Alex, decided to adopt when they found out he wasn't able to have children. When they... passed, six months ago, I became Morgan's guardian." She tried to sound matter-of-fact, though fresh pain sliced her heart and tears threatened. "So just like that, both our lives changed," she added, snapping her fingers. "I went from being Kelsey Harris the Realtor to Kelsey Harris, Morgan's...caretaker."

"I'm sorry for your loss," he said, before he pointed at her. "Oh, snap. You're that Kelsey? You're the Realtor who sold me my house."

Thanks to the internet, she was able to work with clients remotely. About six weeks back, she had sold a five-bedroom house, two doors down from where she lived, all without ever meeting the owner or his agent.

"Yes, I am. And you must be Zachary Johnson?" She leaned forward, feeling more comfortable in his presence. "It's nice to put a face to the name."

She had conducted most of the transactions with his agent and hadn't seen Zachary Johnson. What mattered was that his check had cleared the bank. The commission from that sale was already spent. Two words: Disney World. She couldn't wait to see Morgan's face at that news.

"I just moved in a few days ago," he said.

Kelsey chuckled. "I know. I saw your moving truck." He raised a brow, so she explained. "I live two doors away from you."

"Wow. I would say that's a coincidence, but I know there's no such thing with God. We were designed to meet. Of all the towns in the world, I end up here on the same block as you. That could only mean one thing."

What? What did it mean? Kelsey didn't want to assume she understood his thought pattern. She gestured for him to continue.

"God wanted the girls to meet. This was His

divine ordinance. I would say He has a plan, and I can't even venture to guess what it is."

Her eyes filled. "I think you're right." She lowered her voice. "If I seem emotional, it's because up until today, my niece hasn't spoken much… I don't know why I'm telling you this." She stopped and touched a hand to her chest. Why was she divulging so much to a stranger?

Then his words settled in her mind, and her eyes widened. "You don't talk like a regular person. You sound like a preacher. Like my daddy." She cocked her head. "Are you a minister?" He gave a jerky nod and rubbed his head like her question made him uncomfortable. "I'm sorry. It's just that you reminded me of my father just now. Your tone. Your words. I am—I was a preacher's kid. He was the pastor here at Millennial before August Reid took over."

"I used to be. I… I resigned." He coughed. "I'm not a minister anymore." He pulled on his slacks and fussed with his shirt before glancing around the room. Then he held up the papers in his hand as if they were a lifeline. "I'd better finish filling these out." He stepped away to answer a call before returning to scoot his chair up to the edge of Sienna's desk to complete the sign-up process.

Oh, yes, he was definitely on edge about his resignation. There was a story there. But he wasn't her man to read. She would leave that up to his wife. Kelsey waited until he was done before she changed the subject. "Look at them," she said, pointing to the girls, who were huddled side by side. Mia had an arm around Morgan. "You'd think they had known each other forever. No one would believe they just met this morning. It's unbelievable."

His face softened into a smile. "They must be twins, probably separated during the adoption."

Kelsey's voice box squeezed closed. Hearing the words *twins* and *separated* in the same sentence made her chest tighten.

Zach's brows rose to his forehead. "They are exact replicas. We'll need to take a—"

Just then, the door cracked open and Sienna walked in, fanning her face. Kelsey smiled, glad for the interruption. She was pretty sure Zach had been about to suggest DNA testing. It was the next logical step.

"It is too hot out there for words." Sienna retrieved three small bottles of water from her minifridge and offered one to each of them.

Kelsey declined but Zach accepted, downing his water in two swallows.

"How are you two making out?" Sienna asked. "I imagine this must be a shock to both of you." Then she addressed Kelsey. "You know who is going to have a field day with this?" Sienna rolled her eyes.

Despite the bizarre events of the morning and even though she was still in shock, Kelsey laughed at Sienna's exasperation. Sienna spoke of their town's reporter and one of their childhood friends, Joel Armstrong. He was tenacious when he was after a story and had been determined to feature Sienna in the paper when she made Teacher of the Year. Her friend was equally determined to avoid being in his presence.

Sienna came over to where they sat. "Joel's going to have this on the front page. I guarantee it. I don't know who he has for spies, but I'm certain he's going to turn up here."

Kelsey laughed at Zach's quizzical expression. "Possible twins in Swallow's Creek is big news. The only other set of identical twins are in their sixties, and they are in the *Journal* on the regular."

"Welcome to small-town life. Are you ready to see your daughter in the paper? 'Cause he's going to be at your door, begging for an exclusive." Sienna tapped Kelsey on the shoulder. "I don't think Morgan's going to go for that."

Zach shrugged. "I was a minister of a large congregation back in Philly. The church has an active social media page, so I'm used to the spotlight, though I'm not personally on any social platforms. When my wife and I brought Mia home, Mia's face was all over the page. The town paper will be a breeze for her. When she sees a camera, she goes into fierce mode." He chuckled and then jutted his chin in Mia and Morgan's direction. "They're doing well," he observed.

Kelsey appreciated how he had maneuvered into a new topic of conversation. She was still upset with Joel for putting her sister's accident and her and Morgan's grieving faces on the front page. Once was enough.

"Look at them. It's like they have a special connection," Sienna said. Her words brought Kelsey out of her musings.

"A connection that time and distance has done nothing to thwart," Zach murmured, like he'd already accepted they were twins.

"Their relationship hasn't been confirmed," Kelsey felt the need to point out, touching her chest.

Sienna continued like Kelsey hadn't spoken. "I think they will be fine here together. Since Mia is new and, for obvious reasons, already attached to Morgan, I can put them in the same group. I can always call if they become agitated," she suggested.

When Morgan giggled at something Mia said, Kelsey faced them, and her heart constricted. Her ears welcomed the sweet sound of Morgan's laughter. This time Kelsey couldn't stop the tears from sliding down her face. She didn't want Zach to become curious about her display of emotion, so she jumped to her feet.

She wiped her palms on her pants leg. "I should go. Call me if Morgan gets upset. I only have one client to meet with later this afternoon."

Zach stood when she did. "I'd better get going, too." He called out to Mia, who ran over to give him a hug.

Kelsey walked over to Morgan and wrapped her arms around her niece. "Are you going to be okay?" she whispered close to Morgan's ear.

Morgan nodded and pointed. "Mia's my friend."

She was more than a friend, it seemed. Kelsey knew she was going to have to get some questions answered. But in this moment, she reveled in the blessing of Morgan talking. Holding back more tears, Kelsey said, "Yes, she is. She'll be in your group, so you can show her around so she knows what to do."

Morgan straightened and nodded with solemnity. Zach held open the door for Kelsey, and when she walked out of the office, her heart was light and filled with hope. And, if she were honest, disbelief.

Zach scurried after Kelsey. She had raced out of the center with the speed of a cougar chasing a rabbit. But she was no match for his longer strides. His brain and heart were on overload, and she was the one person who could understand what he was going through. This morning's curveball had whacked him in the chest and disrupted his peace. He felt like he had left one tumultuous situation at his past church in Philadelphia and moved right into another. The quicker he got things settled, the better.

He caught up to Kelsey just before she got into her car.

"Are you free to talk?" he asked. "This morning's events have thrown me off-kilter. I could use a processing partner, and we can get some questions answered." He had gotten a phone call that Sandy's car wouldn't arrive until sometime after noon, so he had more than enough time to eat.

She chewed on her lower lip before giving a hesitant nod. "That's fine. I know we live down the block from each other, but I'm not comfortable having you into my home or going into yours."

"I get it. I just need to talk. How about we meet at Mr. MacGrady's on US 13? That is, if you're available?" Zach had seen the mom-and-pop diner and had decided he would check it out. This was the perfect opportunity.

"That sounds like a plan. I didn't eat this morning, and Mr. Mac's is the best breakfast spot in town." She smiled, and he was caught by how that transformed her already beautiful face.

"All right. You take the lead."

She bobbed her head. "I'll show you a short-cut. I didn't use it this morning because there was a fender-bender, but it should be all cleared up by now."

Twenty minutes later, they entered Mr. Mac-Grady's. Zach loved the hanging metal sign on a distressed wooden post. He held the door so Kelsey could enter first. The restaurant was small and cozy, and a huge chalkboard covered one wall. The rest of the walls were lined with license plates. Light gospel music sounded in the background. He liked the relaxed vibe and easygoing atmosphere.

"Welcome to Mr. MacGrady's," a small, wiry man called out as he bustled by carrying a stack of oversize pancakes.

Zach's mouth watered at the smell of fresh-brewed coffee and pancakes. Kelsey waved a hand before putting her fingers between her lips and letting out a shrill whistle.

"Heyyyy," the staff called out.

A couple diners punched their tables.

"That's how we do it here," she said. "Before we leave, you've got to sign the chalkboard. All newbies got to make it known that they wuz here."

Zach grinned. "All right, bet. I'll do that."

"You going to your usual spot?" one of the ladies on staff asked.

"Yup. You know what I want," Kelsey said, waltzing through the place like her name was on the deed. She made her way around some of the smaller wooden tables to a spot in the back. The tables were all dressed with checkered tablecloths and small vases holding plastic flowers. Once they were seated and had ordered, the waitress brought them two mugs of fresh-squeezed orange juice.

Zach excused himself to wash his hands. When he returned, he noticed her fingers traced a place in the wood that had her name etched on the edge.

"I see you marked your territory," he said in a tone meant to put her at ease. He didn't want to tackle the heavy conversation on an empty stomach. She followed his lead.

"I sure did," she said. "My sister and I claimed

this table. Every Wednesday evening, we would come here with our parents and order burgers and huge milkshakes. Mr. Mac would get on the mic, and the entire diner would play bingo. I'm telling you, I have the best memories in this place at this very table."

"I can only imagine. I would have loved to have your childhood. I've got to remember Wednesday is bingo night."

"Sadly, they haven't done that in a while. Mr. Mac died about five years back. His son, Matt, took over." She drummed her fingers on the table. "There has been so much death these last few years…"

Her face took on a faraway look, and she lost her smile. Zach found himself wanting to revive it. "Are your parents still here in town?" he asked.

She shook her head. "My father and stepmother—well, my mom. She's the only mother I have ever known. My father married her when I was eight months old. Anyways, they sold their house and bought an RV to travel across the country. But that adventure got old really fast. They made it all the way to Florida, then sold the RV and moved to an assisted living facility. Swallow's Creek had too many memories of Kennedy and they were suffocating under them. I stayed. I like the memories," she said, her eyes glistening.

Her voice held pain. Old pain. Fresh pain.

Zach curled his fingers to keep from putting his hand on hers to offer comfort. He had only met her a couple hours ago, if that. Making physical contact might offend her. Instead, he made his face reflect his sympathy. Then he surprised himself by bringing up Sandy. "I'm sorry for your loss. When my wife died a couple years ago, I thought I would drown under my grief. But I had a daughter who needed me. So, I kept going. One second, one minute, one hour at a time."

She put a hand to her mouth. "Your wife is... Oh, I'm sorry, I didn't know."

Zach felt the usual discomfort at talking about Sandy in the past tense. "Turns out you can get cancer more than once" was all he could say.

Fortunately, their food order arrived, sparing him the need to continue. He had selected a waffle with coffee, and Kelsey had ordered scrambled eggs and wheat toast with peppermint tea.

Kelsey excused herself to wash her hands, then they blessed their food and dug in.

After a few minutes, Kelsey said, "So, what are the odds both girls would have names that start with *M*?"

"We didn't name her," Zach rushed to explain, glad she hadn't pried for more details about Sandy. "The adoption agency told us that Mia's birth mother requested we keep her name, so we honored her wishes." He smiled. He could see Sandy's face like it was yesterday, holding the squirmy little bundle in her arms. Mia had been swaddled in a Winnie the Pooh receiving blanket. Zach had taken one look at the tiny little fingers and toes and had fallen in love.

Kelsey took a sip of her tea and wiped her brow. "Kennedy said the same thing when she adopted Morgan."

"I think I know the answer, but I'll ask anyway. When's Morgan's birthday? Mia's is September 26. She'll be six."

"Same."

Kelsey lifted her shoulders before shaking her head. "I'd pinch myself, but I know I'd bruise my arm. This day has been unreal so far."

"How do you think the girls are doing?" Zach asked, eating his waffle.

She tapped her smart watch to look at the time. "They are probably on the playground having a ball." She gasped before yelling out to the waitress for a kid's burger and fries to go.

A rosy hue spread across her cheeks. "I hope you don't mind cutting this short. I promised Morgan I'd drop off her lunch." Pulling out a business card from her satchel, she asked, "I don't know your schedule, but can we meet tomorrow morning at my office sometime to continue this discussion? The address is on my business card."

Zach agreed. "I can head there after I take Mia to camp."

They exchanged contact information, and he settled the tab, insisting on paying for both their meals. Kelsey only relented when he said she could pay next time, then she rushed out the door.

Zach pondered his morning as he drove home. As he strolled up the driveway, the trucker arrived with Sandy's car. Seeing the royal blue Outback glisten in the sun made him miss her more. Once it was off the lift, Zach signed the papers, then opened the garage door and parked her car inside. He touched the steering wheel. Sandy had loved this car, which was why he hadn't wanted to part with it.

Zach exited the vehicle and headed into the house, sauntering through the laundry room and making his way down the hallway to the staircase. The movers had unpacked everything according to his specifications. Then the cleaners he had hired made sure the house smelled fresh. A lemon scent teased the air, and he sniffed. Good. That meant the freshener on the air filter was working.

He slipped out of his oxfords, leaving them on the large mat. So much had changed since he had stepped outside that morning.

Zach moved into the kitchen and looked around. Everything gleamed. He loved the calming grays on the walls and floors with splashes of blue on the backsplash to accent the room. Heading over to the stainless steel refrigerator, Zach eyed the printed schedule for the week.

He had a thin magnetic cup on the fridge where he kept his colored pens. Choosing a red one, Zach wrote, "Twin?" under today's date in cursive.

Rocking back on his heels, he mulled over the implications that came from that one word in red. He rubbed the area between his eyes as thoughts whirled through his mind. If Morgan was Mia's twin, that would require life adjustments. A reconfiguring of the order he had painstakingly established in his life. Lifting a hand, he touched the small photo of Sandy on the refrigerator. If she were here, she would have rattled off a brilliant game plan.

He would have pulled her into a joint prayer session, asking God's guidance. He banged a fist on the metal and shook the scene out of his mind.

That wasn't his life. Not anymore. God had

taken his wife, and no amount of praying, faith and fasting had changed that. Zach still loved God; he just didn't trust Him the same. But he did trust science. And if the DNA testing confirmed what his eyes and heart were telling him, he would find a way to handle it. To cope. His way.

Chapter Three

The birds chirping at 5:30 a.m. outside her window were the first sounds that greeted Kelsey the next morning as she lay in bed. As usual, tears filled her eyes. Another day without her sister. Another day filled with doubt.

She dabbed at her eyes and covered her mouth to suppress her yawn, trying to process the events of the prior day. In less than twenty-four hours, her life had morphed into what would become its new norm.

Turning on her side, she glanced at the ten-inch baby monitor screen to see if Morgan was still asleep. Since Morgan often cried out during the night, Kelsey always made sure it was on. Last night had been quiet.

Morgan lay on her stomach, her braids scattered on the pillow. One leg was off her toddler-size bed, and the other was on. It was time to get her a bigger bed. Kelsey was considering a queen or two twin beds for whenever Mia slept over. Morgan had already asked about that when Kelsey picked her up from camp yesterday.

Anticipating that the girls would want to travel together soon, Kelsey picked up her cell phone, pulled up her shopping app and ordered a booster chair for Mia. It would arrive by 6:00 p.m. that day. Since it was still very early, Kelsey tried to close her eyes to see if sleep would return, but it was no use. Her mind was up.

Might as well get started with her day.

Kelsey reached across the king-size bed littered with laundry she had neglected to put away, listing papers, her trusty crossword book and her rose-gold laptop. She scooted up on the bed and opened her laptop, pulling up her calendar. She had three showings and a closing later that day.

Swinging her legs off the bed, Kelsey slipped her feet into plush pink slippers, averting her gaze away from the pile of clothes seeping out of the laundry basket. She needed to hire a housekeeper. But to do so would be admitting she was failing at motherhood.

She trudged across the shaggy carpet to the master bath to begin her morning routine. It had been hard to move into this space, knowing this had been Kennedy and Alex's oasis. But she had renovated and redecorated using bright colors and sharp contrasts, which helped somewhat. The more the months wore on, the more she understood why her parents had left.

Days like yesterday deepened how much she missed Kennedy. If she were here, Kennedy would have known what to do when an apparent twin popped up, slicing away at the roots of their mundane lives. Dread wouldn't be rolling around on her insides, spreading like a virus, disrupting her entire system.

Once she was dressed, Kelsey awakened Morgan. Her niece's first words were "Am I going to see Mia again today?"

As if on cue, a text from Zach came in. GM. I know it's early, but Mia wanted to talk to Morgan. Is she up?

Yes, but she's getting dressed, Kelsey responded. I can have her call in a few.

Okay. Thx.

When she told Morgan the plan, her niece moved faster, excitement in her eyes. "Can Mia come over?"

"No, honey. But you'll see her at camp later."

Morgan asked again several times if Mia could come over "for a teeny-tiny eenie-weenie bit." Saying no to that pleading face was one of the hardest things to do. But her house was in shambles. She couldn't invite Mia over and have Zach see the house in this state.

Once Morgan was dressed and seated at the kitchen table for breakfast, Kelsey FaceTimed Zach using her iPad so the girls could talk.

He greeted her with a huge smile. "Forgive the early-morning text, but Mia was bugging me all morning to talk to Morgan." She could hear the television going in the background.

"Same here, but I had no problems getting Morgan dressed, so I have Mia to thank for that." They shared a laugh before Kelsey added, "I ordered an extra booster chair, because you know they will want to ride together soon."

His brows shot up. "Good idea. I'll do the same."

Kelsey smiled. "Okay, I'll put Morgan on. She's about to have breakfast."

"Mia, too." She placed the iPad on the table so the girls could chat while they ate.

Kelsey marveled at how Morgan ate more than normal, following her sister's lead. That, along with an even better, uneventful drop-off, had her smiling during the ten-minute drive to her office.

She pulled up to the small storefront.

Seeing the newly painted Harris Realty sign

made her heart swell. Even though it was a little after 9:00 a.m., Sasha must already be inside, because the lights were on.

Kelsey opened the office door, appreciating the scent of fresh-brewed coffee. She sauntered into the waiting area, where she had personally laid down the mauve tiles after watching You-Tube once the landlord had given her permission to tear up the rotting, stained carpet. She'd also spruced up the area with a large piece of wall art, a couch and two armchairs.

Sasha's desk was up front, near the bathroom. Behind her were the file cabinets and a small walkway that led to Kelsey's modest office.

"Good morning," Sasha said, holding out a mug filled with coffee, her purple-painted lips wide. She was dressed in a flared skirt, her ever-present thick heels and a T-shirt. Sasha added to her look with chunky bracelets and chains. "Now, before you panic and get all worked up, I want you to know everything is going to be all right."

Kelsey frowned. She knew this was a small town, but word of Morgan's alleged twin sister had traveled fast. She placed her bag on one of the chairs. "How did you hear about it so fast?"

Sasha rested the cup on her desk and flailed her hands. "Well, it's hard to miss when it's right across the street. Gerald Moore is moving in, and that bright neon sign is out to blind my eyes."

It took a minute for Kelsey to process that Sasha wasn't talking about Morgan.

Gerald was her competition and a major annoyance. Kelsey spun around and crept to the door. Then her mouth dropped at the words *Divine Realty.* "Oh, no. How can he do this? Why is he opening his real estate business right across from mine?" Tension spanned across her shoulders, tightening her muscles. She massaged the back of her neck.

"You know why. He's trying to intimidate you. I heard he bought that entire block." Sasha came to stand next to Kelsey, smelling like vanilla and coconut. She curled her lips. "That snake got some nerve bringing God into this when he knew he did that on purpose. Ooh. He's such a hater. I can't stand haters. But I'll have you know that what God has for you is yours. You don't need to worry about somebody trying to get what's for you."

Kelsey shook her head. All because she'd refused to go into business with him. Gerald was all about the dollar—pushing people toward a home way above their price range. She was about the people. Helping them find the home of their dreams. And keep it. Kelsey backed away from the door and walked in a daze toward her office.

"Are you going to be all right, boss?" Sasha asked with concern ringing through her tone.

Kelsey gave a nod, but she kept her back turned until she entered her office and closed the door behind her. She sighed. "It's too much, God. Too much."

The almost accident.

The twin sisters possibly separated at birth.

The daunting repercussions of DNA testing.

And now, this.

She sank into her chair and clasped her hands, needing to give everything to Him. Because if she didn't, she just might scream.

Zach kept his eyes on the road while he fielded more questions from Mia about her relationship with Morgan.

"Who is she, Daddy?" Mia asked.

"I think she's your sister," Zach said.

"She looks just like me."

"Yes, she does. That's what it means to be twins." He wasn't sure how much she understood but did his best to explain.

Mia nodded. "Was she 'dopted like me?"

"You mean *adopted*." Zach nodded. "Yes, she had a mommy and a daddy, too. Just like you do." Zach and Sandy had never hidden the fact that Mia had been their special gift from God. They had explained the story of Moses and how he was loved and raised by Pharaoh's daughter, just as Mia was by them.

"But Mommy is gone to Heaven."

His heart tightened, and he swallowed. "Yes, she did, honey." He could hear the sadness in his tone, though he tried to hide it from Mia.

"Is Ms. Kelsey going to be my new mommy?" she asked.

He almost stomped on the brakes but kept his voice light. "No, honey. That's not how it works. Ms. Kelsey is Morgan's aunt, and I'm your dad."

Marveling at her question, Zach ground his teeth. He had no intention of finding another wife. He would be friendly with Kelsey because of their daughters' association, but that was all it would ever be.

He frowned, gripping the steering wheel.

Did Mia's question mean she wanted a new mom? He knew there were certain things that a girl needed from her mother, however, he didn't want to put his heart out there again. There was no substituting what he had felt for Sandy. And with love could come loss. She had been taken away much too soon. He buried the traitorous thought that he was beginning to feel lonely and missed having conversations with someone over age five.

"But if she's my sister, won't you be her dad?" Mia persisted.

He peeked at her through the rearview mirror. From her expression, she appeared puzzled, so he strove to explain. When he couldn't come up with a response, he said instead, "I'm happy being your dad." Then he asked, "Don't you like being my daughter?" To distract her from this awkward conversation.

"Yes," she giggled. "You're the best daddy in the world."

"Better than chocolate ice cream?"

"Way better," she snickered.

He continued asking silly questions to make her holler, but her earlier questions stayed in the recesses of his mind. So, when he opened the door to the camp and watched the two girls run into each other's arms, squeezing each other tight, Zach felt a pang hit his heart. Joy and love were etched on their faces. The girls would need each other forever. And he would do all he could to help foster their relationship.

That's why, when he entered Kelsey's real estate agency, Zach felt a fire within him to unite the girls. After introducing himself to the young woman at the front desk and confirming that Kelsey expected him, he followed her directions to Kelsey's office. Knocking on the door, he heard her call out to enter.

The first thing he noticed was her red, puffy eyes. The second was the precarious pile of paper on one side of her desk, threatening to fall to the floor. There was a small book of crossword puzzles on top of the pile. Judging from the condition of the pen cap sticking out from the center of the book, Zach would say she chewed on it while solving the puzzles.

"What's wrong?" he asked, dropping into the chair across from her.

She gave a small shrug, letting her tears fall unheeded. "Everything. That's what's wrong."

He lifted the box of tissues that was on the edge of the desk, careful not to disturb the stack of papers, and offered it to her while fighting his natural inclination to comfort. He wanted to hug her, to tell her everything would be okay. A huge protectiveness overshadowed him as her tears punctured the dome shielding his heart.

"I know you said everything, but what's the major thing that's bothering you?" he asked in a gentle tone.

She wiped her cheeks and rubbed her nose. "What happens if we confirm Morgan and Mia are sisters?" She hiccupped as fresh tears began to fall.

In a swift move, Zach shot to his feet and went around the desk to pull her into his arms. She curved her body into his, sobbing into his chest. He inhaled the light scent of strawberries and gave her a soft pat on the back. "We'll deal with it. One day at a time."

"I can't lose her," she whispered.

Realization hit him with full force. He pulled away. "You think I'd try to take her from you?"

"Why wouldn't you? The girls are going to want to be together, and of the two of us, you have more experience being a parent." She shook her head. "I'm learning as I go. You wanted a child. I ended up with one because of tragedy."

His heart melted like ice under the sun. A sudden urge to cradle her into his chest again seized him, and he backed away, returning to the chair he had vacated.

"Let me put your mind at ease," he said, clearing his throat. "I have no intentions of pursuing custody. The thought never entered my mind." He dared to reach across the desk and cover her hand with his. A jolt of awareness zapped him. He moved his hand and tented his fingers, ignoring the tingles from the short contact.

She wiped her face with a fresh tissue and drew deep breaths. "Okay. Thanks for saying that. I guess I'm overreacting, but I love that little girl like she's my own."

Zach smiled. "Of course you do, and believe me when I say you're not overreacting. You're behaving just like any mother would if her child is in distress."

Her harsh intake of breath suggested his choice of words had startled her. She fussed with the tendrils of her hair, trying to recapture the curls in her bun. "No. I'm not her mother. I'm just her aunt."

He took in her spiked lashes and her high, flushed cheekbones. He doubted Kelsey could be *just* anything. Even in her distress, her beauty shone through. He focused on the abstract art behind her desk, chastising himself once again for being taken in by her physical appearance. But in his defense, the pull wasn't simply physical. Maybe because of their auspicious circumstances, he felt...connected. He stiffened. Any connection needed to be severed.

Zach stood and gave a dismissive wave, a physical attempt to swipe away at the emotional web building between them. "How about we arrange to get the DNA testing done?" He sounded gruff and abrupt, but it was necessary to establish early on the parameters of their interaction. Draw the proverbial line.

She straightened and gathered the papers, tapping them on the desk to align them in a neat stack, then said, "I'll contact Dr. Bowers. She was my pediatrician, and now she's Morgan's. She'll know what to do."

Her voice sounded steadier, but he steeled himself from reacting to her shaky hands as she made the call and set up the appointment for Monday, June 20, at 8:00 a.m. Zach pulled up the notepad on his phone and recorded the doctor's name and the appointment information, tuning out Kelsey's sniffles.

Friendly but impersonal, he told himself, even as his heart protested.

That's how it had to be.

That's how it would remain.

Chapter Four

Kelsey opened the hallway closet and searched for the lavender rain jacket she had purchased on sale at Target. It was a little after 7:30 a.m., and it had been drizzling on and off most of that Sunday morning, which had made getting out of bed more difficult. Of course, now that she was about to leave, she could hear the patter of raindrops. She was only going to Jade's house across the street, but she wasn't about to get her hair wet. Not when it had taken her a couple hours to straighten her unruly curls into this smooth mane.

She didn't see her jacket on a hanger. It must have fallen. Groaning, she bent to dig her way through the paper towels and toilet paper she kept stashed on the floor of the closet. Finally, she saw a flash of color and pumped her fists. She retrieved her jacket before pushing everything back inside and using her body to close the door.

Her phone buzzed in her back pocket. A quick glance showed it was Sienna texting her in the group chat, which consisted of Kelsey, Sienna and Jade. Since they all had iPhones, they had labeled their group The Divas.

Where are you?

On my way, she texted back. Jade responded with a GIF featuring a woman doing an elaborate eye roll.

Whatever. Two Sunday mornings out of each month, the three friends got together to start their week with devotion and to catch up, rotating at each other's houses. Kelsey paid Izabella to watch Morgan while they met. This week was supposed to be Kelsey's, but she had begged Jade to host because she hadn't had time to clean her house.

"Aunt Kelsey, my mom said to hurry up," Izabella called out from the family room, emitting a loud yawn. Kelsey knew Izzy often stayed up past midnight on the weekends, which would explain why the teen looked and sounded tired.

"Really? Your mother is so impatient. I already told her I was on my way. She must forget that I have a young one—correction, make that two young ones, to feed before I can get dressed." Mia had slept over, and Kelsey had done their hair in identical styles and dressed them in similar colors—at their request. They had fallen asleep watching *The Parent Trap*, a movie Kelsey had admired as a child.

Zach sent a text. Is 10:00 am good to come get Mia?

Yes. Izzy is watching both girls. You good with that?

That's fine. Text me her number, please.

Kelsey sent him Izzy's contact information. The teen had already turned on the television and was flipping through the channels.

As she slipped into her jacket, Kelsey heard a loud bang and rushed to the bottom of the stairs. "Are you girls all right?" she called out.

"Yes, I'm showing Morgan how to do a flip," Mia shouted back.

Izzy came to stand next to her and patted her on the arm. "You go. I've got this." She took off her sneakers and ran up the stairs.

Kelsey cocked her head and listened. Hearing light giggles, she yelled, "I'm leaving."

Of course, no one responded. She slipped the hood over her head and ventured outside into what was now a heavy downpour. Her umbrella was in the trunk of her car, and Kelsey figured she would be okay without it. A minute later, she entered Jade's home drenched, her hair wet and puffy. Shrugging out of her jacket, she slipped off her water-soaked wedges. She could already smell the almond pretzels Jade had purchased. Her mouth watered. Blessed with a high metabolism, Kelsey usually ate two.

"Here you go," Jade said, holding out a towel with one hand and a mop in the other. Kelsey must have looked a fright, because Jade's mouth dropped open. "What's going on with your hair?"

"It got ruined in the rain," Kelsey explained, raising a hand to her head. She thanked Jade for the towel and wiped her face before blotting her hair.

"You look like you had your hand in a socket." Her friend touched her own edges as if to assure herself that her hair was still on point. And, of course, it was. Jade's pixie cut was well-behaved. "I'll get you a scrunchie or something when I'm done," she said with sympathy, then proceeded to mop the water off the floor using rapid strokes, her bangles rattling on her wrist.

She wasn't sure where her petite friend found that energy, but this was one morning she wished she could buy some. Kelsey knew from experience Jade would reject her offer to help, but she did anyway, and of course, she received the same response. While she dried her legs, she took a moment to admire the buttercup-yellow A-line dress against Jade's smooth mahogany skin. The contrast made her beautiful friend even more striking. Plus, Jade was one of the few people who could wear lipstick colors like yellow and green and make them look trendy.

"These smoothies are going to be water by the time you two make your way in here," Sienna said from the kitchen.

"I'm coming," Jade said. "I just need to wash my hands."

"I hope you didn't get me anything with bananas in it," Kelsey said, sauntering into Jade's oversize kitchen and heading to snatch one of the pretzels. She took a bite and licked her lips. Jade must have gone to Patty's Pretzels early that morning, because they were still warm.

With the wraparound bar with ten chairs, granite counters, deep cherry soft-close cabinets and stainless steel appliances, this kitchen was every cook's dream. As a personal fitness trainer, Jade spent many days concocting treats to help her clients live a healthy life while eating well, so she'd invested a lot of time into making sure this space fit her needs.

"Girl, after all these years, you think I don't know how you like your smoothie?" Sienna shot back.

Kelsey kissed Sienna on the cheek, giving her arm a light squeeze. Sienna was dressed in blue jeans, Chuck Taylors and a black blouse. Her nails had an interesting cow design.

"I know. I just like pushing your buttons. That's all." She reached for the small cup of pineapple-mango smoothie and took a sip. "My stomach thanks you."

Her eyes went wide, zeroing in on Kelsey's head. "See, that's why I get braids. You won't ever see me with my hair looking like I'm related to Albert Einstein."

She couldn't help but crack up at the analogy. "That's why I'm avoiding the mirror."

Jade returned with the promised scrunchie. Kelsey wrapped her curls in a bun before washing her hands.

"Now, let's get down to business." Jade picked up her smoothie, climbed onto one of the high bar stools and rubbed her hands together. "Tell us all about you and Zach."

"Me and Zach?" Kelsey arched a brow and took a seat. "I thought we were going to talk about Romans 12? I made sure to get that reading done before going to bed last night."

"Yes. We will," Sienna said, coming to sit

beside Kelsey. "But first, we want to know all that's going on with the two of you."

"I heard he's single," Jade said, waggling her brows. "A widower. And he's great with the girls."

"There is no two of us. He was very much in love with his wife. And need I remind you of why I haven't dated since Christian?" Kelsey slurped her smoothie. Christian Miller had been a client she had met eighteen months prior who proposed after three months of dating. The night he asked for her hand was the night she ended things.

Jade sighed. "No need. Dating leads to marriage and marriage leads to kids." She repeated Kelsey's often-spoken words verbatim.

"I keep telling you, you've got to let that go. Your mother dying after childbirth wasn't your fault. Blame that on the doctor who refused to treat her hemorrhaging," Sienna said. "Plus, I've got news for you. You already have a child."

"My sister's child," Kelsey emphasized.

"Your child," Sienna corrected. "And Morgan now comes with a sister."

"Don't forget the fascinating daddy," Jade added.

Kelsey cocked her head at Jade. "If you find him fascinating, why don't you date him?"

Jade drummed her fingers on the countertop. "I think I've had enough of the love and marriage thing to last me a lifetime. Don't you agree?"

Kelsey's and Sienna's eyes met. Of the three, Jade had been the only one to get married, have a child and get divorced. Her ex-husband's name, Ralph, had been banned from being uttered. He had the face and body of a model, but his heart was like coal.

"I don't blame you," Kelsey said. "Sasha recommended I try a dating site. Girl, I told her that it was not for me. Just the other day, I read about a married police chief caught dating three women. It was all over the internet. He posed with his wife, telling Facebook how much he loves her, while telling those three women he was divorced."

Sienna shook her head. "Yep, that's why I'm leaving men alone. It sounds cliché, but I'm good all by myself. I don't need a husband when I have you two. We're the Three Divas, all for God, for life. Besides, I already have a second love, with God being the first—my computer. It's never let me down. Frankly, I don't have time for anything or anyone else until I finish my dissertation. And for all I know, God could mean for me to be single." Sienna was a doctoral student at Wilmington University and would present her dissertation that fall. She snapped her fingers. "I'm not lonely or unfulfilled, and I'm at the peak of my career. What more do I need?"

"Go on, Ms. Teacher of the Year for the second year in a row." Jade and Sienna high-fived.

"Joel missed the chance to put that in the paper," Kelsey teased.

Sienna rolled her eyes. "Don't get me started on that man. He's a nuisance." She went to get a cinnamon pretzel.

"Speaking of Joel, he's coming by to interview us and the girls tomorrow," Kelsey said.

"We all knew that was coming," Sienna said. "But in this case, I have to agree that the girls meeting each other like this is big news."

"Yes. Their finding each other is more than a coincidence," Jade chimed in.

Kelsey shifted. Zach had pretty much alluded to the same thing, but she wasn't about to think about that too hard.

"Let's get back to the original conversation," Jade said to Kelsey. "Tell me you haven't noticed how fine he is."

Kelsey shook her head. "I have eyes. Zach is…pleasing to look at." The man was swallow-the-drool fine, but she found his thoughtfulness more endearing. But Kelsey knew better than to admit that to her friends. "My attention is on Morgan and Mia. These last couple days have been about them. They want to be together all the time. Zach and I have been—"

"Zach and I?" Sienna arched a brow. "That sounds like a couple to me."

Kelsey redirected the conversation to a much safer topic. "I don't care how it sounds. It really is about the girls. We're juggling them between us. Tomorrow is the DNA testing. Though we both believe it will be a confirmation of what we already know, it'll be good to have scientific proof. Let's add that to our prayers today."

Jade nodded and picked up her phone. "I'll add it to my prayer app."

Sienna tapped Kelsey on the shoulder and gave her a pointed look. "Some things don't need confirming. Some things we already know."

He wasn't one to share.

Zach knew he could be territorial.

But in this instance, he had no choice. He had to share his baby girl, his sole companion and road partner, with her sister. Zach had allowed Mia to spend the night at Kelsey's. Her first sleepover. Something he normally wouldn't have allowed days after meeting someone, but he trusted Kelsey and her choice of a babysitter. He had met the teen the day before, and Izzy appeared to be sweet and capable. Besides, if anything arose, he was only a couple of doors down.

Zach drank some of his coffee and opened the sliding door to head into the sunroom. He had already finished his workout, showered and dressed. The pitter-patter of the rain on the roof soothed him. He finished his coffee and returned to the kitchen to rinse his cup and put it in the dishwasher.

Glancing at his watch, he noted he had a couple hours before he was due to get Mia. Zach went down the hallway and entered his workroom. In the center of the room was a large oval table. Against the wall in the far corner, he had mounted two large storage boxes, each with thirty-two compartments, that he had purchased from Lowe's. Below them were two smaller plastic compartments that held Mia's Legos and art supplies. She had a mini work desk in the corner, along with her easel.

Since he was a child, Zach had loved basketball and Legos. If he wasn't dribbling a ball, he was building things. Now that he was grown, he had moved on to building model cars. The kits had about thirty-seven hundred pieces that came sorted in separate baggies, costing close to $300. He kept them in storage bins until he was ready for them. Zach had installed shelves and had three of his collectible cars on display.

Mia's Lego cars were right beside them. He slipped onto the chair behind the table where he had the parts to what would become a red-and-black convertible.

Slow. Steady. Carefully, he worked on the model until his cell phone buzzed with a text from Kelsey.

My pastor wanted to reach out to you. Welcome you to town. Do you have a problem if I give him your number?

He had known this was coming. Inevitable, really. Yes, that's fine. Thx for asking.

He then returned to work. His cell rang. Surprised to see an hour had passed, Zach answered the call. He didn't recognize the number, but it was a Delaware area code.

"Is this Pastor Zach Johnson?" a deep baritone asked.

His stomach tensed. "Yes, this is he." It had been a minute since he had been addressed with his title. This must be the pastor calling.

"I'm August Reid, the pastor of Millennial House of Praise."

"Oh, yes. My daughter attends your summer program," Zach said, scooting deeper into his chair.

"I've heard about the twinsations, and I can't wait to see them for myself."

"They are causing quite a stir in Swallow's Creek. As a matter of fact, they're going to be headlining the town's paper." He tapped the leg of the table with his foot.

"That would be Joel Armstrong's doing. He keeps our town informed, and twins separated at birth is major news," the pastor said with a chuckle.

"Yes. It's unbelievable. I wanted to wait until the DNA results, but Joel is very persuasive. He's coming by tomorrow at 6:00 p.m."

They shared a laugh and other pleasantries. The pastor asked how he was settling in before offering to stop by to bless his home. He joked that Zach probably had that handled before changing his tone.

"I won't beat around the bush," Pastor Reid said. "I'm hoping if you're looking for a church home, you'll consider coming to help me at Millennial House of Praise. We're a congregation of about two hundred members, and we're full of love and all about family. I know you were a bigwig in Philly, but we would love to have you. I would love a man of your experience to break the word and to help mentor the youth."

The pastor was saying all the right words— the youth had been Zach's heart. He cleared his throat and rubbed the bridge of his nose. "You know I appreciate you reaching out, Pastor Reid—"

"August, please," the minister interrupted.

"Okay, August. I'm so glad for your call, and this town has been welcoming. I feel Mia will blossom here. But when it comes to church and God and ministry, I don't do that."

There was a pregnant pause. "Don't do what?" August asked.

"Religion. Faith. None of that. I resigned from all that."

"Resigned. I see," the pastor said. Zach hunched his shoulders, preparing for a spiritual sparring similar to the one he had had with his ministers in Philly. But the pastor simply continued, "If you weren't already a preacher, I would be bringing you the Word, but you wrote books I study on the subject. How about I stop by and pray with you sometime this week instead?"

Zach couldn't open his mouth to reject prayer. "I won't turn down anybody who wants to put me up before God. However, it won't make a difference. My mind is made up. I won't commit to serving that way."

"I hear you. I hear you." The disappointment in the man's tone made Zach feel a twinge of guilt. But the pastor wasn't done. "I tell you what. I'm starting up a basketball summer league, and I know you have the skills. I looked you up. Not too many people know you played overseas before you got the call to ministry. Would you consider spending some time with our young men? They could use a positive male image. They need to see other brothers doing the right thing. You know what I'm saying?"

Of course he did. He had been one of those youth. He had needed a mentor to guide him and keep him off the Philly streets. Zach had been fortunate to have a coach who pushed him into minor league basketball. He would have still been on the court if God hadn't grabbed him first.

"I can do that," Zach found himself saying. "That I can do."

"Great. That's good to hear." August sounded jubilant. "The boys are going to hit the roof when I tell them about this. When can you start?"

Zach looked at the model car and shrugged. "Give me a day or so to arrange my schedule. In fact, how about Thursday? I'll pop over to the church after I drop Mia at camp so we can meet and finalize the details in person."

"All right, bet. Thursday works for me. Sounds like a plan. See you then."

Once the call ended, Zach held the phone in his hand. He had mixed emotions about what he had just committed to do. But regret was not one of them. He had earned a good living in basketball and in ministry, and sadly he'd inherited a good sum of funds upon Sandy's death. Zach was also skilled at investments, so he wasn't in financial need. However, his mind was at a deficit, and he wasn't employed. Helping the young men would be a way to fill his mental tank while doing good.

Yep. For the first time in a while, Zach felt anticipation.

He walked into the kitchen and added his meeting with August to his calendar on the refrigerator. Another date jarred his peace, zapping through his heart, leaving him hollow. July Fourth. Zach's stomach knotted. It was fourteen days away. He rested his head against the fridge and closed his eyes.

July Fourth.

Independence Day.

A day for many to barbecue and have fun. But not for him. For him, Independence Day was the day he'd lost his wife and his faith for good.

Chapter Five

At 7:58 Monday morning, Kelsey pushed open
the door to the pediatrician's office, hiked her
bag high on her shoulder and held on to Morgan's hand. Memories of her skipping into this
office with Kennedy when they were children
flashed into her mind. Her eyes watered, and
she sniffled, her legs becoming heavy to lift.

Morgan trudged behind her, wiping her own
eyes with her free hand. Kelsey had dressed
her in a pair of jean shorts, a purple T-shirt and
light-up sneakers. The sneakers were the only
things that fit right. And of course, there was
her Princess Tiana backpack.

Once they were inside, Kelsey released her
grip and allowed Morgan to go play by the
dollhouse in the corner. No one else was in the
waiting area, but the television was already on,
with *Moana* playing on the supersize screen,

although the volume was down low. She walked up to the reception area and wrote Morgan's name on the notepad, all the while thinking about how this was Kennedy's job. Annette, the assistant, wasn't behind the glass door, so Kelsey took a seat.

The doctor's office had two entrances and waiting rooms, one for sick patients and one for well visits. Kelsey loved that idea. She didn't need Morgan intermingling with the other children and getting sick. She settled in the seat, taking in the ocean theme—the child-friendly sea animals dancing on the wall, the sound of the bubbles from the fish tank.

Then the door opened, and a small whirlwind entered dressed in pink tights, a matching leotard and a tutu. Her father followed behind and lifted a hand in greeting before going to the window to check-in. He was dressed in a black shirt, tan slacks and loafers. Since she had a client after this appointment, Kelsey had chosen navy blue pants with mauve stripes, a matching mauve blouse and a pair of chunky navy blue heels.

"Hi, Ms. Kelsey," Mia said, running over to give her a hug and a kiss on the cheek.

"Hey, little mama," Kelsey said, shaking off the web of sadness and hugging her close. In four days, Mia had found a firm place in her heart.

Mia broke contact when she spotted Morgan. The girls hugged and rocked each other. Their display of love made Kelsey teary-eyed. She noticed that Zach stood watching them as well. He held his phone up to snap a few pictures, sending copies to Kelsey.

"I'm so glad you were able to get us in today," Zach said, coming over to where she sat. He had paperwork to sign, stating he had filled out the papers online to enroll Mia as a new patient. Kelsey thought his using the same physician for his daughter was a smart choice. He propped the clipboard on his leg and gave her a warm smile before signing his name with bold strokes.

Being the beneficiary of his smile made her insides flutter. She crossed her legs, careful not to snag her heel in the green carpet. "Yeah, Dr. Bowers agreed to see us before her first patient at eight fifteen."

He sat next to her, a waft of ocean and musk filling her nostrils. If it weren't for Annette calling out to her that Dr. Bowers was ready for them, she might have done something silly like tell him she loved the scent of his cologne.

Mia and Morgan held hands, chattering the entire time, with Mia driving the conversation. The walls were filled with dancing children and toys that enticed the girls along the way. Annette led them into the first room, placing a couple of charts into the bin. Kelsey smiled at the large poster of a dancing seahorse.

"I love the atmosphere here," Zach whispered in her ear.

The low rumble of his voice made its way down her ear canal. "You'll love Dr. Bowers even more. I promise."

Dr. Bowers had to be close to seventy, but you wouldn't know it. She was of Peruvian descent, and her hair had remained dark and full. Dr. Bowers always had lollipops in her pockets, which made Kelsey's mouth water like she was six years old again. The doctor stood by the door and gave a little wave before reaching for the charts, then she strolled in, greeted them and washed her hands.

Kelsey hugged her before introducing Zach. Since the twins were going to be there anyway, Kelsey had scheduled Morgan for a checkup, and Zach had asked for the same for Mia as well. Once she was done checking their vitals, Dr. Bowers would swab their cheeks and send the vials off to the lab.

"Hello, girls," the doctor said, doing the Chicken Dance. "I'm Dr. Bowers."

Mia and Morgan twisted their bodies, mimicking the physician. "Hello, Doctor," they said in unison.

Dr. Bowers stooped to their level. "Nice to meet you."

Morgan frowned and shook her head. This wasn't her first visit and Kelsey wished Morgan would verbalize that.

The doctor studied both girls before covering her mouth. "Oh, my."

"We look alike." They said the words together again.

Kelsey felt her brows raise as goose bumps popped up on her arms.

"How are they doing that?" Zach asked, his eyes wide.

The doctor asked the girls all kinds of funny questions while she took their temperature, weighed them and checked in their ears and inside their mouths. Giving a nod, she asked Zach about Mia's immunization records. He handed her a physical copy. It turned out both girls were due for a second dose of the MMR.

"I don't…" Morgan began before her chin trembled. Kelsey jumped to her feet to comfort her niece, though she knew how this was going to go.

"Want to get a shot," Mia said, finishing Morgan's sentence.

"It's a tiny prick," Zach said.

Together, Zach and Kelsey held the twins while Dr. Bowers delivered the shots. Kelsey was prepared when the doctor began to sing a funny jig at the top of her lungs right before sticking the needle in their arms. The girls were so busy laughing, they didn't feel the prick. Kelsey hid her grin at the marveling on Zach's face.

"I told you she was good," Kelsey whispered while Dr. Bowers swabbed their cheeks. Zach managed a nod, but she could see he was charmed. "She's taken, so you can't marry her," she teased, pulling on Zach's arm.

His face shuttered for a moment—though she could have imagined it—before Zach tilted his head back and laughed.

Zach's cheeks hurt from laughing. It was an alien sound. He couldn't remember the last time he had laughed so much or felt so relaxed. What a blessing this was. Coming here with Kelsey and Morgan had made a routine visit fun.

The four of them piled out of the examination room, he and Kelsey on separate ends and the girls in the middle. By then, the waiting room had filled with other parents and their children. A couple of the moms smiled at them, probably making the natural assumption that they were a family. He fought the urge to shout out an explanation. They exited the doctor's office and went over to their vehicles. Zach had parked his truck next to Kelsey's car.

They stopped between their vehicles. The girls stood with their heads together, whispering and giggling. Zach tried to hear what they were talking about, but then Kelsey addressed him.

"Mia looks adorable in her tutu," she said, wiping her brow. It was going to be a scorcher. Maybe a black shirt wasn't the best idea for this heat. He could feel sweat running down his back. He would change once he got home.

"It's her first day of gymnastics—I have her scheduled for Mondays and Wednesdays—and she insisted on wearing her leotard to camp today. I didn't want us to be late this morning, so I added the tutu and rushed over here," he explained.

"I hope you bought another set just in case." She must have noticed how Mia handled her clothes.

"Yes, she has sets in purple, green and every other color of the rainbow. I like to be prepared." He could see the approval on Kelsey's face and grinned.

Mia came over to Zach, tugging her sister behind her. She pulled on his leg. "Daddy, Morgan wants to ask you something."

Zach gave Morgan a smile, but she placed a fist in her mouth, her eyes wide. He bent low so he was on her level. "Yes, sweetie. What do you want to say?" He noticed Kelsey had an expectant look on her face.

Morgan glanced at Mia, who held out her hand in encouragement. "Go ahead, Morgan. You can ask him. It's okay."

Her little chest puffed, and she whispered. "Can I go to gymnastics with Mia?" From the corner of his eye, he saw Kelsey dab at her eyes, but he had to give Morgan his full attention.

"That's great, Morgan," Mia said, beaming at her look-alike. "You did it."

Morgan gave a little smile and rocked from side to side, the straps on her backpack dragging on the ground. Zach reached out and took her hand. Then he asked, "What did you say? You have to speak a little louder so I can hear you." He wanted to see if she would repeat her words. Kelsey hovered close.

"Can I go to gymnastics with Mia?" she asked again, this time in an almost-normal tone. Zach's eyes met Kelsey's, and he raised a brow at her in question.

Her eyes shone and she nodded, this time not hiding her tears. The joy on her face made him catch his breath. Kelsey was looking at him like he had scored a three-pointer from beyond the arc.

"Of course you can, honey," he said, patting Morgan on the back. "You can wear one of Mia's outfits."

"Good job, Morgan," Mia said. She voiced the words with the same tone and inflection he used when praising her. Zach was so proud of his daughter, he snatched her close, stood and lifted her in the air. She squealed with delight. He then did the same with Morgan, loving the sound of her shy laughter. As soon as he put her down, the girls held hands and jumped with glee.

"Ms. Kelsey, can you buy us matching outfits?" Mia asked. Of course, Morgan nodded, agreeing with her.

Zach opened his mouth to protest. He had taught Mia better than that, but Kelsey's head bobbed with excitement, so he held his tongue. "Let me talk to your dad about it, first. Okay?" The girls' faces were brighter than the sun. Kelsey's next words explained her quick response.

She placed a hand on his arm. "I've been trying to get Morgan to let me get her some new clothes. Meeting you two has been the best thing for Morgan." She didn't give him a chance to reply before moving on to ask, "Did you sign her up at Shining Stars?"

"Yes, how did you know?"

"It's one of two in town. I took a chance," she said with a giggle, moving her hand, unknowingly leaving her imprint.

"Her class begins at four thirty and goes until five fifteen."

"Before the accident, Morgan was in ballet lessons. She refuses to go back no matter how much I plead with her. So gymnastics is a good start." She pulled up her phone to look at her calendar. "I'll stop by there after my appointment and get her signed up."

"Great. We can go together if you want." Even as his mouth formed the words, panic closed around his lungs like a zip tie. He rubbed his neck, his admonition to remain friendly but distant ringing in his head. Going together would suggest they were a family. A unit. But they weren't. They needed to be more like Lego pieces, coming together and easily taken apart.

"Sure. It makes sense. I have a feeling the girls would want to ride together anyway." Her practical tone eased his concerns. Maybe he was overreacting.

She flicked her wrist and looked at her watch. "I've got to get going." She opened her car door and called out to Morgan.

"Can she come with us?" Mia asked. "I want to ride with my sister."

"Yes," he said without consulting Kelsey. Realizing his mistake, he whispered an apology. By now, his arms were feeling toasty under the sun's rays.

She waved him off. "No worries. I have to go to the other side of town anyway, so you'd be doing me a favor."

He pressed the button to start up the truck so the air conditioner would come on. Then he opened the passenger door. Mia scampered inside with Morgan behind her. He turned to ask Kelsey for Morgan's booster seat and found her already bent over in her car, reaching for it. "Thank you. The one I ordered arrived, but I forgot to put it in my truck."

Avoiding eye contact, he made sure their hands didn't touch when she passed over the new booster seat.

She fanned her face with her hands. "I wish I had time to get a lemonade from Patty's. She makes the best lemonade in town."

Zach grinned. "You sold me. What's her place called?"

"Patty's Pretzels. It's right off Main. You can't miss it."

"I'll take the girls there before dropping them off at camp."

"Great. I'll order pizza for after gymnastics. I know just the place. Las Ortalanos has the biggest, cheesiest slices ever." She smacked her lips.

"Later?" he asked, furrowing his brows.

"Remember Joel is coming to do his exposé on us—rather, the girls?" she asked, squinting up at him while shielding her eyes from the sun. "Did you forget?"

"No. That's right. He's coming by my house at about six tonight. So, yeah. Pizza is good." He gathered his scattered thoughts. Having Kelsey peer up at him like that was distracting. Sort of.

"Perfect. See you then."

They parted ways, and after getting the girls settled in their booster chairs, Zach looked up the shop before telling the girls his intentions. He turned around when they shouted with glee. His heart constricted. He could have been both girls' father.

No reason why I couldn't be now. A mental image of the four of them leaving the doctor's office flashed before him. That could be his new normal. If he was the dad, then that would make Kelsey...

No. No. And no, again.

His throat tightened. Panic flared. That spot was reserved for Sandy. He shoved that traitorous image out of his mind. Then, ignoring the sight of the girls holding hands, their identical faces beaming at him, Zach backed out of the parking space.

Chapter Six

Kelsey fumed. Oh, she remained professional, with a wide smile, but on the inside, she was all hot lava. She stood next to her clients, Xuan and Tai Nguyen, in a six-bedroom, six-bathroom beach house located in Rehoboth Beach. The foyer was comparable to the lobby of a five-star hotel. Her left eye twitched as Gerald Moore walked his clients through the very same property. The place was listed at a steal price of $800,000. She had heard the owners were older and motivated to sell. If Kelsey sold this forty-two-hundred-square-foot home, it would be her highest commission yet.

Etiquette dictated that Gerald wait until she and the Nguyens had departed before coming inside, and he knew it. Gerald had to have seen their vehicles, but he had intruded during the middle of her tour. The fact that he had shown up here during her appointment, an hour away from Swallow's Creek, told Kelsey this was no coincidence. Oh, Gerald had put on a big show to apologize, claiming he had mistakenly double-booked, but she knew him. This was intentional.

"I'm sorry about this," she said, gripping her file. "It should only be a minute."

Tai smiled and said, "It's okay, dear. We understand this can happen."

But that was the thing. It should not have happened. She counted to ten. Her cheeks hurt from trying to keep her smile in place.

"We already know we love the house from the virtual tour. But seeing we have potential competition makes me want to put our bid in now," Xuan said. Kelsey loved the lyrical sound of their Vietnamese accents. The Nguyens owned several pet shops across Delaware and were eager to move closer to their parents.

Grateful for their patience, Kelsey took several short breaths to calm her temper.

"I agree," Tai said.

"Okay, we can do that." Kelsey gripped her satchel and led them into the big, airy kitchen to set up her laptop on the marble-topped island, which boasted a second dishwasher—yes, a dishwasher and a spectacular view to the ocean. But even with its mint-green cupboards and top-of-the-line appliances, this impressive room paled in comparison to the supersize laundry room. Kelsey and Tai had oohed and aahed over the double sink, the double washers and dryers, and the chocolate-colored folding table.

With quick strokes, Kelsey pulled up the electronic forms to complete their bid. She had pre-filled in everything but the house information. The couple linked their arms and waited. Kelsey felt a pang. This was her third time house hunting with them, and their love for each other was evident. Xuan was so solicitous, holding the door and at times kissing Tai on the cheek or rubbing her back. And these were not newlyweds. They had been married for nineteen years.

For the first time, Kelsey admitted she wanted that. Love. Marriage. She just didn't know how she would tackle the issue of not wanting to give birth to a child.

"Let's offer more than the asking price," Xuan said, breaking into Kelsey's thoughts and quoting a generous addition.

"Are you sure?" Kelsey asked.

"Yes. We want to be sure we get it."

"All right," she said, adjusting her numbers. Taking out her portable printer and placing it on the island, she activated the hotspot on her cell phone and pressed the print button. Once the Nguyens signed, she would stop by the office and fax the papers over to the Realtor.

By this time, Gerald had returned with the young couple behind him. He cleared his throat as if to say she should leave, but Kelsey lifted her chin and ignored him. She felt the heat of his eyes on her back and straightened. There was no way she would allow him to see how his presence affected her. Gerald took them through the kitchen quickly before heading to the laundry room. From where they stood, they could hear the other couple's gasps. She gritted her teeth. If she lost this deal because of Gerald, she didn't know what she would do.

She dug in her bag for her special pens—ones she reserved for clients and that weren't chewed on from when she did her crosswords. Then she showed the Nguyens where to sign.

Tai must have read her mind. "Before you send it, we pray."

Xuan nodded, his hair moving with his movement. That was the second thing she liked about the Nguyens—they weren't afraid to share their faith. That was the reason they had signed with Kelsey, saying they like the Scriptures she had on her website. Kelsey held out her hands. They joined hands, and Xuan uttered a quick prayer.

"It's in God's hands now," Tai said with an eager smile.

Twenty minutes later, while she drove home on Route 1, she remembered Sasha had told her that the fax machine had been acting up. Kelsey would need to stop to purchase a new one at Staples before they closed. She called Zach, who was watching both girls and getting them ready for gymnastics.

"Hey, I have to make a quick stop before coming to meet you guys for gymnastics." She explained the situation with the fax machine. "I don't want to miss the girls' first class, but I promised my clients I would get this bid in tonight."

"Why don't you stop here and use my fax machine?" he suggested. "Then we could travel together. The girls would like that."

"I don't want to put you out," she hedged. She didn't want to start depending on Zach for random things in her life. His being there for the girls was one thing. Helping her was another.

"It's no problem," he assured her. "Friends can help each other out."

He was right. Kelsey had no reason not to accept his help. "Thank you," she said. "I'll be there in about a half hour."

"See you then."

Once she ended the call, her text notification sounded. It was Gerald. She pressed the play button on the dashboard so that her car would read the text aloud to her.

My clients want that house so no use bidding on it.

Kelsey rolled her eyes and gripped the wheel. She wouldn't answer him. Gerald took satisfaction in rattling her and playing childish games. Well, she would follow Michelle Obama's example, to which she had added her own twist: when he went low, she would go *higher*.

Pitiful.

If he could sum up his actions right now, that's the word Zach would use. Here he was, pressed against the wall outside Mia's room to keep from being spotted, and eavesdropping on his daughter and Morgan's conversation.

"I wish Ms. Kelsey could be my new mommy," Mia had said.

Those nine words made him question his parenting and his decision to remain single and left him with his heart hammering in his chest. That's what he got for listening in on their conversation.

Zach had placed the laundry basket down and was now waiting for Morgan's answer. He had to remain quiet so he could hear her much softer tone.

In his defense, he had been about to saunter in with Mia's folded laundry when he heard the words that made his legs feel wooden. He had picked up the girls from camp, made them wash their hands and sent them both upstairs to change into leotards for gymnastics. Mia had returned home with holes in her tights, stains on her leotard and a shredded tutu. And her hair. Her hair. The braids had unraveled, leaving it all askew. Camp life must be rougher than he thought. But then, Morgan still looked presentable, so it must be Mia. His baby played rough.

"But she's already my auntie," came the quiet reply.

He placed a hand over his mouth to cover his chuckle. He wished he had brought his phone with him to record this conversation. Kelsey would have enjoyed hearing Morgan speak at least five words.

"I know, but if she married my daddy, then we would be together."

On second thought, perhaps it was a good thing he wasn't recording this. He didn't know how Kelsey would react.

"I want us to be together," Morgan breathed out.

"Then tell Ms. Kelsey to marry Daddy," Mia

said, before using one of Zach's expressions. "It's that simple."

What a little smarty-pants! Zach's eyes went wide. If she weren't plotting his future, he would have been delighted at her tactics. He had a future attorney on his hands.

"I—I don't want to do that," Morgan said. He heard the sound of drawers being opened and closed.

He pumped his fists. Morgan might be quiet, but she was no pushover. His daughter, however, was persistent.

"You've got to. I know you don't like to talk, but how else will Ms. Kelsey and Daddy know that we want to live in the same house? Didn't you say you want us wearing our hair the same and wearing the same clothes?"

"Y-yes," Morgan said, sounding uncertain.

"So you have to do it," she pleaded.

"But what if she don't like him?"

He furrowed his brow. Morgan's perceptive question amazed him.

"Everybody likes my daddy," Mia shot back.

Zach decided it was time to end this matchmaking session. He whistled loud enough so they could hear, picked up the basket and entered the room.

"Look, Daddy, we're putting on our clothes." Mia held up the leotards and smiled such an innocent smile that if he hadn't heard her blatant manipulation, he would have been charmed.

Biting the inside of his cheek, Zach nodded. He placed the pink basket near her bed. Mia would put away her clothes in their respective drawers and return the basket to the laundry room, as he had taught her. "Okay. Hurry up and get dressed. You don't want us to be late for your first gymnastics class. Ms. Kelsey is coming to meet us."

The girls started undressing, and he hurried out the door and rushed into his master suite to freshen up. Unlike the rest of the house, he hadn't taken the time to decorate his surroundings. He kept the design functional and minimal. The large area boasted his king-size bedroom set, a large mounted television and his computer set up in the far corner of the room. Zach did utilize both walk-in closets. One for his clothes, and the other held storage bins. Bins full of pictures and other keepsakes from his marriage. He had chosen to decorate his house with abstract art and Mia's pictures, keeping one picture of Sandy on display on the wall to the right of his bed and another on his nightstand. Mia had more pictures of Sandy in her room.

While he changed his shirt, he mulled on Mia's words. His daughter really wanted to be closer to Morgan. And she would gain a mother in the process. Something he knew she must yearn for. He understood that need because God started the world with two people who eventually became parents.

That's why Zach didn't get why God had taken Sandy away from him. He went into the bathroom to brush his teeth. Turning on the faucet, he gripped the sides of the sink. But if he hadn't lost Sandy, he wouldn't have ended up moving, and Mia wouldn't have met Morgan. He couldn't regret that. If he were honest, he couldn't regret meeting Kelsey, either. He just wished she would stop invading his mind at the oddest of times.

Like right before she called. He had been thinking of her, wondering how she was making out with her clients and if she would make a sale.

His cell rang from inside his bedroom. That was her calling again. See? He had been thinking about her again. He pressed the button to accept the call.

"It's pouring out here, and traffic's backed up. I'm going to exit as soon as I can and go on 13."

"No problem. Stay safe. We'll meet you at gymnastics, and I'll make sure to remind you to send the fax after we're done."

"Thanks," she said, sounding relieved. "That sounds like a plan."

Zach pressed End.

Then he froze.

Their conversation sounded like one between a husband and wife. Like one between a couple.

He shook it off. He was overreacting. Friends helped friends who needed to send a fax. That's all it was. Nothing more.

Chapter Seven

Before going into the gym, which was technically a warehouse, Kelsey sprayed vanilla mist in her hair and clothes. It would have to do. She tossed the small bottle back in her glove box and dug into her bag for some gum. She wished she had a chance to shower and change, but she didn't want to miss Morgan and Mia's first day of gymnastics. Zach and the girls were already inside.

Opening her door, she stepped out in her flip-flops, having ditched her heels in the back of her car. Her feet were happy to be free from their clunky confines to show off their fresh manicure. The rain had died down, and it was hot and muggy again. Fall couldn't come fast enough for her.

She turned her head from side to side, stretching her muscles. The day had been long, and she was ready to go home. Decompress. She had been tempted to call Joel to reschedule their meeting, but he had said he wouldn't need more than twenty minutes.

You know what, she would text Joel and see if he could stop by the gym and do the interview there. Snapping her fingers, she reached into her pocket for her phone and sent the message. Within seconds, Joel responded that he would stop by.

Looking at her watch, she could see that it was 4:43 p.m. She closed her door and headed inside. Girls of all ages and sizes were on balance beams, the bars and the floor. Kelsey stopped at the front counter to pay Morgan's fees and complete the registration process. Then she headed up the stairs to join the other parents. She stopped at the head of the stairs. Almost every chair was occupied.

Her heart rate escalated when she saw Zach. He had been looking out for her and gestured to the chair next to him.

"Thanks so much for saving me a seat," she said, slipping into the metal folding chair.

"No problem," Zach said.

She made sure to put her phone on silent while she observed the session.

Beside her, a mother held on to a squirrelly toddler who was crying to join his sister below.

His little foot thumped Kelsey on her leg. The woman apologized, but Kelsey assured her she was fine.

"How are the girls doing?" she whispered to Zach.

He pointed to a corner of the room. "They're stretching now, and the instructor had to tell Mia to stop talking."

She chuckled and followed the direction of his finger, spotting them sitting together. Her mouth hung open when she saw Mia's hair. It looked like it had encountered a tornado. She wouldn't comment, choosing instead to talk about the positive. "Aw, they look so cute." Kelsey watched them do some floor routines. Mia performed her flips like a champion. "She's really good," she said to Zach, holding on to his arm.

"Yes, she bends her body like it's putty."

His muscles tensed under her touch, but she didn't release her grip. She was too enthralled with Morgan's handstand.

From behind her, a shadow loomed. She felt a tap on her shoulder and jumped. She whipped her head around to see who it was before she relaxed.

"Hi, Joel. I'm glad you're here."

Joel was about six foot four, lanky with dark

curls and a mustache he'd refused to shave since high school. He was dressed in a pair of jeans with a short-sleeved dress shirt and his ever-present baseball cap. Kelsey knew that behind his unassuming appearance was a man of great intelligence, with his perfect SAT score—which annoyed Sienna to this day.

A large camera hung around his neck. He gave Kelsey a kiss on her cheek and waved to Zach. "Thanks for inviting me. I think I'm going to get some good pictures. I also brought a videographer with me." Joel meandered his way through the crowd and found a spot in a corner.

She removed her hand to pin her hair in a knot, retrieving a ponytail holder from her purse. "I hope you don't mind me having him come here instead. I figure we can kill two birds with one stone."

"Why do we have to kill them, though?" Zach asked, finally resting those spectacular eyes of his on her.

She scrunched her nose. "Kill who?"

"The birds."

It took a moment for his words to register. Kelsey didn't know if it was because she was tired, but his words tickled her. She fell over with laughter, continuing to laugh until tears rolled down her face. The other parents glared at her, but she couldn't control herself. Maybe she was more exhausted than she had thought. Or it could be because Zach was laughing right along with her.

A flash before her eyes snapped her out of her fit. She looked over to see that Joel had taken their picture.

"What are you doing?" she demanded, rising out of her seat. "You said you needed a picture of the girls. Not me."

He shrugged. "I loved the connection I saw between the two of you. I'll send you the picture." With that, he was off.

She sat down and addressed Zach. "Didn't that bother you?"

He shook his head. "It's just a picture." But it wasn't. Not to Kelsey. Pictures didn't lie, and she didn't know what was on her face. Because she was beginning to like Zach Johnson. A lot. And in an unguarded moment, she might have shown it. She chewed on her bottom lip. She wasn't ready to admit that truth to herself, much less to have it made public.

"I'm not worried about it. Are you?" Too distracted to wait for an answer, he pointed to the girls. "Whoa. Look at Morgan on the balance beam. She's a natural."

Kelsey nodded and forced her attention back on the girls, where it should have been the entire time. She scooted her chair away from Zach a couple inches and hoped he hadn't registered her retreat.

Zach didn't know if he had done or said anything to change Kelsey's mood. It seemed as if one minute she had been laughing, and the next, she had put distance between them.

He had noticed, but he hadn't asked because he had been determined to keep things neutral in their interactions. That meant keeping his mind focused on the girls and not allowing Kelsey's change in demeanor to affect him— although he loved to see her laughing. It meant commanding his heart rate to beat at its natural rhythm, and it meant pretending the moment Joel had captured of them together was no big deal.

Slow and steady.

That was his mantra, because Zach was too aware of everything Kelsey.

When the session ended, Joel sauntered over to them to snap photos of Zach and Kelsey with the girls. He had obliged but had made sure to stand next to his daughter. Zach had battled feelings of relief and disappointment when Kelsey did the same.

Kelsey then followed him home and took a

few minutes to send off the fax. When her cell vibrated, she dug it out of her purse.

She groaned. "That was the seller's agent. We've been outbid." He could hear the disappointment in her voice. She hunched her shoulders. "Let me text the Nguyens." She fired off a text, her fingers moving fast.

Zach curled his hands, surprised at how tense he felt watching Kelsey texted back and forth with the Nguyens. He was rooting for her to make a sale.

"They want me to go higher," she breathed out. Kelsey completed a new bid and faxed the offer over to the agent.

When it was time to say their goodbyes, Mia and Morgan protested. The girls hadn't forgotten about the promised pizza. Kelsey had already ordered pizza for delivery at her house, so they decided to eat there. Zach and the girls decided to walk over while Kelsey backed out and pulled into her driveway.

Mia and Morgan raced the short distance. He didn't know how they had so much energy after the rigorous workout at gymnastics.

"They're going to sleep really well tonight," Kelsey said, walking to her front door. "Let me warn you that my house isn't in the best of conditions. I'm only allowing you in here because you're almost fam." She opened the door, and the girls scampered inside.

If her house was anything like her desk at work... Zach lifted his hands. "I understand the life of a busy single parent. I'm not here to judge. I'm here for the free pizza."

She chuckled. "Humph. You're not following me. Your house is a showpiece." She beckoned him inside.

"Thank you." He tucked his head to his chin and stepped across the threshold, steeling himself not to react to what he might see. He looked around the vast living area. Scanning the gray fabric couch, the china cabinet and the coffee table, he could see where a little dusting was needed, but nothing looked out of place.

She lifted her chin. "Did I pass inspection?"

"It's not as bad as you make it sound," he said. Above his head, he could hear the girls running about, but Kelsey didn't seem to mind. "They sound like squirrels."

Motioning for him to follow her, she went into the kitchen. He stopped, unable to hide his surprise at the dishes, the containers and the laundry. Zach was tempted to fill the double sink with water and start washing up.

"I told you," she said, not looking him in the face. "In my defense, I've been swamped, and by the time I'm done, let's just say I'm not motivated to do housework."

His heart melted, and he yearned to give her a hug. "I get it. Listen, superheroes only exist on television and in the movies. Not in real life. I'm able to keep my house clean because, A, I have a schedule, and B, I have the luxury of time, so quit being hard on yourself." The word *schedule* reminded him of something else he'd meant to discuss with her. "Mia and Morgan's birthday is a few months away, so I was thinking given the circumstances, we probably should coordinate that together."

She raked her fingers through her curls. "Oh, I've got that on lock already. I'm taking Morgan to Disney World. It's a surprise. I can't wait to see her reaction. She's going to be so cute wearing those Minnie ears." She whispered the words, and he could feel her excitement zinging off her like fireworks.

Intense disappointment hit his core. Zach knew Mia would want to be with her sister on their birthday. And she wasn't the only one.

Fortunately, Kelsey said, "Maybe Mia could come with us?"

Just Mia? Before Zach could answer, she rubbed her chin. "But I'm sure you want to spend her birthday with her, too." She tapped her feet and lowered her eyes. "Uh, maybe this is something we could, um, do together?"

"That would be wonderful," he said, trying not to be fascinated by her flushed cheeks. "I was planning on taking Mia soon anyways. But going the week of their birthday means they would be missing school."

"Don't you know birthdays are a holiday?" She opened the dishwasher and began loading it.

Zach moved to sit at the kitchen table. "I'm not following."

"We skip school and work for birthdays in this house. Besides, it's first grade. Morgan reads at a third-grade level, and her math skills are already close to fourth grade. She won't miss much."

"Do you need help?" he offered.

"Naw. I've got this." She strutted around the kitchen, putting things in order with speed and efficiency.

Zach wiped his brow and thought about his structured life. Nothing was out of place. Ever since his wife's death, his entire day was planned down to the hour. He hadn't been able to control the circumstances that claimed her life, but he could control how he spent the 1,440 minutes each day.

Slumping deeper in his chair, Zach found he rather liked the notion of a skip day. It sounded liberating. Refreshing. He mulled on this while he ate his pizza. They could let loose.

Later, when he was about to leave with Mia in his arms, he mouthed the words without any hesitation and with a huge amount of anticipation. "Count us in."

Chapter Eight

"Hello, I'm here to pick up the letter from the lab," Kelsey said to Annette through the Plexiglas. She wiped her hands on her jeans and willed herself to remain calm. Even though she had a good idea of the outcome, her nerves were like jumbled wire.

Kelsey had just dropped off Morgan at camp when she'd received the call and had zipped over to the pediatrician's office. Before she arrived, she had called Zach, and they had agreed to meet at his house. She would stop there once she had the envelope in hand.

"Sure, let me get that for you." Annette walked over to the cabinet and began searching through a bin.

Kelsey took that moment to send a text to the Three Divas group.

The DNA results are in.

She watched the three dots signifying someone was typing a response, tapping her foot
while she waited.

Wow. That was fast, Sienna texted.

What does it say? Jade wanted to know.

I didn't open it yet, she fired off.

What you waiting for? Jade asked.

Sienna chimed in. It's not like you don't know
what it says.

Kelsey started to type.

Zach and I—

Then she stopped, deleted and started again.

We—

No, that sounded too couple-like. *Ugh.* There
was no reason why sending a text should be so
complicated.

Sticking her tongue between her teeth, she
tried again.

Zach wants to find out at the same time as I do.

There. That was better. Nothing that could
be misread as something more.

Sienna responded with heart emojis, and Jade sent her kisses emojis.

She looked up from her phone to see Annette holding the brown letter-size envelope with a hand on her hip. After thanking her and blowing a kiss, Kelsey drove back to her development and pulled into Zach's driveway. She grabbed the envelope and hurried out of the car.

Her orange heels clicked against the asphalt as she walked up the three steps to the front porch and rang the doorbell. She cupped a hand against her face and peered through the tempered glass of one of the wrought iron doors. He had replaced the wooden ones, and she liked the new addition. These were the minor adjustments that added value to a home.

"Hey, you," he said, opening the door, sounding super casual. "You nervous?"

"A little bit," she said, wiping her brow. The June heat was already unbearable at ninety-seven degrees. She was glad she hadn't scheduled any clients today. Kelsey planned to spend the day cleaning.

His eyes popped in the sun. She knew it wasn't possible, but Zach seemed to become more handsome each time she was in his presence. She clutched her chest and uttered a low greeting before going inside.

"Let's go into the kitchen. I was just about to

make smoothies. Want one? Unless you'd rather we open the envelope first?"

Patience was something she needed more of, but she found herself saying, "Naw. I can wait. My stomach got happy when you said *smoothie*." Her unspoken truth was that it would give her more time with Zach. It struck her that since meeting each other, this would be the first time they were alone together. Her insides fluttered at that realization.

With a nod, he pivoted and headed into the kitchen. He had a swagger that needed to be copyrighted. She entered and closed the door behind her.

The house had a fragrance. She sniffed. Fresh linen. She looked around. As she expected, it was spotless. There wasn't anything out of place. After admiring the abstract art and stopping to fawn over Mia's portraits, signed with her name in all caps, Kelsey followed Zach into the kitchen.

Spread across the counter were a couple mangoes, several green apples, a banana, a bag of spinach, chia seeds, a Ninja processor, a cutting board, an apple slicer and a Santoku knife. "I don't like bananas in my smoothies," she said, placing the envelope on the counter and washing her hands.

"That's all right. I can do without it."

If he had a problem with her making herself at home in his kitchen, Zach didn't voice it. Instead, he went to the refrigerator and took out cold water and ice.

She chose the biggest green apple and used the slicer to cut it into chunks, then popped a piece in her mouth before putting the rest in the Ninja. Zach came beside her and opened the bag of spinach, grabbed a handful and added it to the pitcher. Her heart lost its rhythm for a second at his proximity before it accelerated. She reached for a mango, aware of him and that he had a fresh-out-of-the-shower smell.

Zach seemed to anticipate her need before she asked and retrieved a paring knife so she could peel the mango. The mango felt full, and the juice ran down her arm. Resisting the urge to lick the juice off her skin, she went to the sink and washed it off instead. Next, he opened the bag of chia seeds and poured a couple of tablespoons into the Ninja.

Kelsey loved how they worked together in silence, not needing to talk just to talk. She didn't think she'd ever felt at ease with a member of the opposite sex before. And she liked it. Zach finished up the rest of the smoothie, and Kelsey went to look at his calendar on his refrigerator. Scanning the sheet, she was impressed at his structure and organization and told him so.

"It's all about developing a system that works for you," he said, pouring their drinks into tall glasses and getting them smoothie straws.

She took a sip before she nodded. "This is delicious."

"It's the date nectar I added," he said. "It's one of nature's sweets." He guided them into the living area and opened up a couple of wooden trays side by side. Zach took a few sips before he placed the glass on the tray and rubbed his hands. "Now, for that envelope. Are you good with me opening it? Or do you want the honor?"

"Go ahead," she said with a wave.

Zach left and returned with the envelope, coming to sit next to her. She felt the couch dip from his weight. Her appetite deserted her. She watched as one long, tapered finger slid under the clasp and tore open the envelope. Her chest heaved. Kelsey reached over to take his hand and tented her fingers with his. They sat holding hands for a few seconds.

"I'm nervous," she confessed, releasing his hand.

"Are you nervous that they are sisters or that they aren't?"

Kelsey shrugged. "I honestly don't know."

"No matter what, we'll be all right and the girls will be in each other's lives." He gave her a side hug before withdrawing the letter. Then, clearing his throat, he read the results: the science did indeed confirm what their eyes and hearts had seen.

Mia and Morgan were twin sisters.

Separated at birth.

The caption read, "One big, happy family." Zach held the town paper in his hand and stared at the front-page photo of Kelsey, the girls and himself. They were smiling, and to anyone who didn't know them, they looked like the poster family for happiness.

He wondered if Kelsey had seen the paper and how she felt about it. After the not-so-surprising reveal yesterday, she had gotten quiet.

Science had made everything more real.

Last night had been the first time since bumping into each other that Mia and Morgan had spent their evening apart. Both Zach and Kelsey had agreed to tell the girls separately about the news.

"I know that already, Daddy," Mia had said.

Kelsey had reported that Morgan had said the same thing but more concisely. Her exact words had been, "I know."

This evening, he had taken Mia to gymnastics, but Kelsey hadn't shown up with Morgan. Mia said Morgan hadn't been at camp earlier, either. Zach hadn't pushed or called. Mia hadn't performed with her usual vigor, confessing she missed her sister. Seeing her downturned lips, droopy shoulders and lackluster performance had tugged at his heart, especially since he was feeling the loss of their presence as well. But he had to respect Kelsey's space.

After giving Mia her bath, he settled her into bed, promising her she would see her sister tomorrow.

His cell buzzed. It was Kelsey. Zach smiled. Not just a regular smile, but one of those big grape-flavored Kool-Aid smiles. He knew it wasn't biologically possible, but even his heart smiled. He answered the phone, keeping his tone neutral.

"Have you seen the video?" she asked, breathing heavily into the line. He tried to gauge if she was okay from her tone. She sounded normal and excited, making his heart happy.

"What video?"

"The girls have gone viral. Joel's interview about them finding each other after all these years has been picked up by national news stations. That clip has been played everywhere. They are calling Mia and Morgan 'twintastics.'"

"No, I haven't seen it."

"We're coming over," she said, ending the call.

Zach raced upstairs into his bedroom and

snatched his iPad off his bed. Then he stopped into the bathroom to brush his hair and rinse his mouth with mouthwash.

"Mia, Morgan's coming," he yelled. He thought he heard a squeal, but then the doorbell rang.

"Hurry up, Daddy," she said, jumping on his back.

Zach scurried down the stairs, making sure to make Mia bounce, loving her giggles. When he opened the door, the girls pounced on each other, ending up on the floor. They rolled around with the energy of lion cubs. Kelsey stepped over them and went into the living room. Zach hoisted the girls to their feet.

"Let's go upstairs," Mia said, dragging Morgan by the hand.

Zach smiled and watched their ascent. All was as it should be.

"She's asked for Mia at least a hundred times today," Kelsey said, sitting in the same spot from the previous day.

He joined her once again. "Mia, too." He rubbed his head. "They can't stand to be apart. Mia said it was like missing a part of her."

Kelsey's mouth hung open. "She said that?" When he nodded, she looked shamefaced. "I'm sorry. I needed to process. I don't know what I needed. But we played hooky today. We slept late. We vegged out on the couch. Ate ice cream."

He lifted a hand. "You don't have to explain." Though he was glad she did.

"But mostly, I spent the day in prayer. There's some stuff at work, too, that had my brain all haywire. I needed to spend some alone time with God to clear my mind."

Sudden loneliness pierced his heart. And, dare he say, jealousy. She had the relationship with God he used to have. Zach had once hungered for God's presence. His guidance. Hearing Kelsey speak made that spiritual thirst rise up within him. But he swallowed it down and focused on the worry in her eyes.

"What's going on with work?" he asked, hoping she would trust him enough to open up.

She shrugged. "I don't want to bore you with the details. I came for us to watch the video together." She reached into her bag for her cell phone.

He should let it go, release his concern to maintain that safe distance. But Zach was tired of pretending he didn't care when he did.

After she played the clip and they laughed and joked about it, he placed a hand on her shoulder. "Tell me what's wrong. I'd like to think we're almost friends."

"Almost friends? There's no such thing." She

chuckled. "We're friends, Zach. When I saw that video, you were the first person I called. The first."

He nodded, his heart feeling light at that declaration. He liked that she considered him a friend. "Okay, friend, tell me what's going on at work."

She blew out a puff of air and squared her shoulders. "Right before I started my own business, this other Realtor approached me about going into business with him. Gerald Moore. He's a big shot, but I feel he doesn't care about people, and he's not honest. He'll sell hardworking people a money-draining property just to make a sale. He's all about profit, and while I do want to make money, I also have to answer to God and live with myself. Since I turned him down, he has done all he can to mess up my deals and to get in my way, even going as far as opening his business right across from mine."

He scrunched his nose. "Say what?" He didn't remember seeing another real estate business when he had gone by her office.

"Yes, it's there. Right across the street. That bright and gaudy sign is on display. Yesterday, after I left here, I got a call from Sasha saying that two couples I planned to sign decided to go with him. So he's poaching my clients just to get back at me. Gerald also outbid me on two properties, and that would be fine if I didn't know he's doing this to undermine me. Fortunately, he wasn't able to succeed in this major sale I made in Rehoboth Beach. I got the word that my offer was accepted." She massaged her temples. "It just got to be too much for me to handle. I knew it was time to put God on the case."

"That guy sounds like a piece of work. I can understand your exasperation." His words were a bit formal, but Zach was fighting his natural inclination to hug her, offer her emotional support.

She snorted. "Exasperation is an understatement. If I weren't saved…"

"It's because he knows you are that he is behaving this way. He knows you won't retaliate."

"I guess…"

She chewed her lower lip. This time Zach couldn't hold back. He gave her a small hug, then pulled away. "Congratulations on your sale." The desire to pray with her was strong. When he was a practicing minister, Zach had prayed for many people but not always with them. Sandy. He had prayed with Sandy. As if she had read his thoughts, Kelsey slipped to her knees and held out a hand.

"Come on. I know you know how to do this better than me," she urged.

Zach looked at her outstretched hand and expectant face. He wanted to, needed to, but he couldn't. He shook his head. She gave him a sad smile before closing her eyes. Then she prayed out loud in a clear voice. For him. For Morgan. For Mia. It was unselfish. Inspiring. Welcomed.

The words flowed from her, and he felt a sweet presence in the atmosphere. Tears filled his eyes. He knew this feeling. Yet the words wouldn't come. He couldn't utter a word of praise. Instead, all Zach could ask was why. The question he had been asking for two years. *Why did You take Sandy away from me?*

Chapter Nine

Her crossword puzzle lay forgotten on her lap, right along with her cell phone. Kelsey had been texting back and forth with the Nguyens, celebrating their offer being accepted. The closing had been set for that Friday. Normally, a closing could take weeks, but both parties were motivated, and since securing a mortgage or going through underwriting wasn't needed, they could conclude business in a matter of days.

Once she was done, Kelsey tried to concentrate on work, but her mind was preoccupied with the therapy session in the far corner of the room.

A picture of the girls at gymnastics, captioned with, The girls doing cartwheels, popped up on her phone.

Glad for the distraction, she sent Zach an

emoji with stars in the eyes. Thanks for sending this. They are so cute.

Mia wants to talk to Morgan.

Now's not a good time. I'll have her call in an hour.

Cool.

She tossed her cell in her purse, scooted deeper into the olive green couch and observed Morgan's interaction with the therapist. Dr. Hernandez and Morgan sat on the floor at the kid-size desk, crayons scattered about them, as Morgan drew a picture of her family. Kelsey drew in a deep breath.

Dr. Hernandez had been skillful at engaging Morgan in small talk. Her niece supplied answers to the doctor's questions—using more than one word. Morgan had been more than happy to share news about her sister. Mia's name had been mentioned numerous times—right along with Zach's.

She had wandered over there earlier to take a peek before the doctor motioned for Kelsey to keep her distance. Kelsey had obeyed, but she'd already seen the beginnings of Morgan's family. Rather than the picture of Kennedy, Alex and

Morgan that Kelsey had hoped for, she'd spotted the outline of two little girls of about the same height, which was sweet. Kelsey swallowed the lump in her throat and wiped under her eyelids. Her niece was already replacing Kennedy and Alex. Maybe it was Kelsey's fault. Maybe she wasn't doing enough to keep them fresh in Morgan's mind. She bit the inside of her cheek as her guilt surfaced.

"Let me know when you're ready for me to look at your drawing," Dr. Hernandez said, holding on to the desk and getting to her feet.

She was wearing bright colors, slip-on shoes, fuzzy earrings and thick-rimmed, rainbow-colored glasses. The headband with floppy rabbit ears completed her look. Kelsey suspected her garb was designed to make the children see her as a friend. The therapy room had a seesaw, bright colorful balls of all sizes, a hopscotch grid and toys for all ages.

After retrieving her notepad, the doctor came to join Kelsey on the couch. She turned sharp, empathetic eyes on Kelsey and asked, "How are you doing?"

"I'm good," Kelsey said, wondering why she was being questioned. This session wasn't about her—it was about Morgan. "How's Morgan?" she asked.

"Your niece seems to be adjusting well. She's

very happy to have a sister. She talked about her a lot."

Kelsey laughed. "I'm not surprised. This past week has been nothing short of amazing. Morgan is opening up, and for the first time, I'm hopeful that she'll be herself again."

"What about you?" The doctor cocked her head. "Morgan told me she thinks you are very sad."

Kelsey touched her chest. "Me?" she asked, even though she was the only other person besides Morgan in the room. She looked over at Morgan and shook her head. "She hasn't said a word."

Dr. Hernandez nodded. "She's worried about you, and I think your grief is a part of what's keeping her from recovery."

What?

A feather could have knocked her out. Her mouth hung open. Kelsey gripped the couch to steady herself. This was her fault? Tears pooled in her eyes. She crossed her legs and faced the doctor. "How am I to blame?" she asked, speaking low enough that Morgan wouldn't hear her. Morgan hummed under her breath, focused on her drawing.

"This is not about blame. This is about moving on the plan God has for you." Dr. Hernandez scooted close and placed her clipboard on the coffee table. She grabbed a couple tissues and handed them to Kelsey. Her eyes held concern, not accusation. "This is about Morgan's healing. And now, it appears, yours."

Kelsey thanked her and blew her nose. "But I'm fine. I'm working. I'm managing. I'm taking care of Morgan—" She sniffed.

"You're functioning," the doctor said, touching Kelsey's arm. "This is a case of what the Bible calls the mote and beam. You're so busy focusing on Morgan—her mote—that you're not paying attention to the wedge in your heart. The beam." She cocked her head. "Let's talk about that, Kelsey. Is there a beam?"

It was like the doctor held the string for the dam to her heart and had made the decision to pull it open. Kelsey unraveled like a loosely knitted blanket. She tensed, tightening her core. But hearing she was somehow keeping Morgan from moving forward, the dam broke open. Her shoulders shook, and she covered her mouth to keep from releasing a full-blown wail. But the cry of the pain buried deep in her soul would not be silenced. Like bile, it had festered long enough and begged for her to purge her system.

"Is there a beam?" That question repeated in her mind, pushing at her heart. With a nod, Kelsey's response was a seal-like groan. She released short, staccato breaths and fanned herself, overwhelmed, overcome, realizing she was about to become undone. She lifted a hand and said, "I need a minute."

The doctor nodded but remained silent. Kelsey closed her eyes, hating to see the pity and sympathy reflected in the other woman's eyes. Jumping to her feet, she staggered out of the room. Kelsey held on to the wall as she made her way to the restroom.

The restroom smelled of lemons and had two stalls. She chose the larger one, rushed inside and locked the door behind her. Kelsey pressed against the door, using her hands to support her weight and keep from falling to the floor. Then she fell apart. She cried and cried and cried. She cried until the bagel with egg and cheese she'd had for breakfast made its way out of her system.

When she was done, Kelsey rinsed her mouth and face, using the paper towels to dry off. She avoided the mirror, knowing her eyes were puffy and red. Then she stood there, debating how she was going to go back in that room and face Dr. Hernandez. She sniffed. *And Morgan.*

Kelsey admitted she didn't want to be vulnerable. She didn't want to examine her inner doubts and inadequacies. Her fear. But she had to.

She couldn't fail her niece. She couldn't fail God, who had placed Morgan in her care. She was all Morgan had. And she had plenty of love for Morgan. Kelsey bunched her fists. Her love was stronger than her fear. Squaring her shoulders, she returned to the room.

Zach pulled into the church's parking lot ten minutes before 3:00 p.m. for his conference with August. A text from Kelsey came through, and his smile was automatic and wide.

Text me when you're done. We will meet you at the mall.

Kelsey planned to take both girls shopping.

Will do.

There was a white F-150 parked in the pastor's spot. August had called to postpone their meeting until today, the first day of July, stating he had had an emergency with one of his parishioners. Having lived that life himself, Zach had completely understood.

Seeing his phone was at 9 percent, Zach left it to charge in his truck. He jumped out of the vehicle, surprised at the eagerness he felt to begin talks about working with the young men. It would be great to pick up a ball again. Zach had all the ESPN channels, but he hadn't kept up with the sport like he had with his Legos. However, that was about to change.

August had told him that he would leave the front door unlocked, so Zach opened the door and stepped into the foyer. There was a guest book on a small round table and a coat closet to his left. Straight ahead there were white double doors, which he assumed led to the sanctuary. He headed right, passing by the huge silk ficus as he had been directed. Turning down a narrow hallway, he passed a lunch area, a children's room and a mothers' room before coming to the last door on the right.

It was cracked open. He could hear August's deep voice on the phone with someone, so he stood outside until the call ended. Then Zach rapped on the door. The pastor waved him inside, standing to greet him.

The first thing Zach noticed was that August Reid was shorter than he'd expected. He had a commanding voice, which reminded Zach of T. D. Jakes, so he'd expected someone of similar build. But August was about five foot eleven, though he exuded the same authority and confidence as the televangelist. The second thing Zach noticed besides the large oak desk with the matching chairs, credenza and conference table was that there was a set of drums set up in the back of the room. Probably a stress reliever.

August came over and greeted him with a hug before giving him dap. Zach had dressed in a pair of slacks, a polo shirt and loafers, which was much more formal than the white shorts, plaid shirt and sandals the pastor wore.

"Let's sit at the conference table," August said. He pointed to a box of doughnuts. "Help yourself."

Zach declined, but August helped himself to a chocolate-covered doughnut.

"I've got to get deliverance from this sweet tooth," he said, patting his stomach and biting into the treat.

Once they were seated, August got to the point. "The six young men we're starting off with spent time in juvie. They aren't bad kids. They just lost their way and could use a kick in the right direction. Everybody needs a second chance sometimes. I volunteer at the correctional center in Smyrna. Two evenings a week, I go and I share the Word, and I talk with them. I check up on them about school, but they need a healthy outlet. And that's where you come in. Their basketball coach quit, so I've arranged with the warden for them to be bussed here. Twice a week, you can coach them, get them to run off some steam."

Zach drummed his fingers on the table. "I've got to say I'm impressed with your vision. I've done some mentoring in Philly, but I never worked with juvenile delinquents."

"I see them the same as any other kid. They need love. That's it. Love them and steer them right." The other man seemed to get heavy in introspective thought before saying, "Let's just say, I could have been where they are if God hadn't called me all those years ago."

He was moved and even a bit envious by August's sincerity. Zach couldn't tell when he had felt that passionate about anyone or anything besides Mia. She was the only one he allowed himself to love and remain in his heart.

"I can hear the devotion and commitment in your voice," he said. "I'm honored to assist you in your vision, and I understand your motivation."

"I love what I do," August replied. "But I confess, sometimes I want…more." The pastor appeared pensive yet again. Zach fought his natural inclination to delve into what that meant. August gave a light shake of his head. "That's a conversation for another time."

August rose and strode to his desk, returning with a sheet of paper. "These are the boys' names and contact information. They range from ages fourteen to eighteen, and they are excited to meet you. I invited them to our July Fourth barbecue, and I was thinking that might be a good time for you to meet them. The warden is releasing them to my care on that day and then again on the eighth. We're rounding out the week with a summer dance. My head deacon, Deacon Rose, and I will pick them up in the church van. You're not cleared to come inside, but you're free to tag along with us."

Zach felt sucker punched. July Fourth. Independence Day. Sweat beads formed on his forehead. He drew small breaths, hating to disappoint August or the boys. He could do this, he told himself. Sandy would want him to help those boys.

August's eyes narrowed. "Unless you've made other plans?"

Yes, if you counted huddling in his bed, watching videos of Sandy and eating pizza with Mia. He forced the words out. "That would be fine." At least he hoped it would be. The dance on the eighth was on a Friday, so he had no conflicts there.

"Tuesdays and Thursdays would be great for me," Zach said, pulling up his calendar on his phone. "My days are open, so whatever time you need me, I can help."

"How about from nine to noon? That way, they can play ball and have lunch. I'll set everything up." August had a huge smile on his face as he stood, extending his hand.

Zach had just lifted his hand to shake August's when August frowned. "Are you all right?" Zach asked.

The other man's brows furrowed, and he began to shiver, clutching his abdomen. Now his face was contorted in pain. August cried out and bent over. When his knees buckled, Zach moved fast, catching him before he fell to the floor.

Chapter Ten

It wasn't like him.

Not that she had known him long.

But the man she was getting to know would have called to check on his child hours ago. Kelsey paced in the living area, chewing on her bottom lip. She had texted, called, but Zach hadn't answered his phone. Eventually, his voicemail box declared it was full. With her messages.

Zach knew she was taking the girls shopping for clothes and dresses for the summer dance. He'd promised to text when he was done with August.

All the while they meandered through the stores and aisles, she had kept her ear cocked for the sound of a text or phone call. However, the mall had closed hours ago, and she had returned to her place without hearing a word. She placed a fist in her mouth and groaned. Something must have happened. She was wearing down the bottom of her slippers, but she didn't care.

It was close to 11:30 p.m., and Kelsey had put both girls to sleep in her bed. They couldn't both fit in Morgan's bed. Mia had asked for her father several times, and Kelsey had had the burden of pretending everything was fine while worry gnawed at her like a field mouse with wire.

Kelsey had reached out to Sienna and Jade, but they hadn't heard anything. She'd even texted Joel to see if he had heard of an accident…a fire…anything. But he had said everything was fine. But everything wasn't fine. If it were, Zach would be home—er, at his place.

Where could he be?

She twisted her hands. This was too much. Slipping to her knees, she began to release her stress through tears. "Lord, I don't know what's going on, but please let Zach be okay." Even as she prayed, she berated herself for being dramatic. For overreacting. If he was all right when he finally got there, she was going to scream. *Ugh.* He'd better be hurt or injured in a hospital after making her fret like this.

She stopped. *A hospital.* Her heart raced, and dread lined her stomach. Covering her mouth, she rushed over to the phone and dialed Bay

Health. When the operator came on, she asked for the emergency department.

She gripped the phone, her hands shaking. "Hello? Clara? Hey, girl. Listen, can you do me a favor? Can you tell me if Zachary Johnson has been admitted as a patient?"

"Only for you, girl," Clara said. She had been one of Kennedy's best friends.

Kelsey walked from one end of the house to the other while Clara searched the records.

"No. I don't see his name."

She massaged her neck. "Are you sure?" Her shoulders slumped. Not that she wanted Zach to be a patient. She just wanted to know where he was.

"Wait. Is he the one who was with you in the paper? The one with the weird eyes?"

Weird eyes? Oh, she must be referring to Zach's different eye colors. *Weird* wasn't the word she would use, though. "Yes, that's him," she breathed out. "Please tell me you've seen him."

"I have seen him."

"This might be asking for too much, but do you think you can put him on the phone?"

Clara paused for a beat, then she released a sigh. "Okay, hang on."

A few tense minutes later, she heard Zach's voice.

"Zach," she breathed out. "Are you all right?"

"I came in with Pastor Reid…" She could hear the worry in his voice. "I'm sorry I didn't call. I left my phone in my truck, and it's still at the church. How's Mia?"

"Slow down. It's all good. I knew you had to have a good reason."

"How did you know I was here?" Zach asked.

Kelsey twisted her hands. "I was worried about you when I didn't hear from you, and I had a full-blown panic attack before God, and yes, I'm saying it was God who put it in my head to call the hospital. I know the nurse who answered, and she said she saw you there."

"Wow." She heard the amazement in tone.

"What's going on with August—er, Pastor Reid?"

There was a commotion in the background before Zach said, "Kelsey, I think I'm about to get word on the pastor. Let me call you back." He rushed off the phone.

Her heart rate increased, pounding in her ear. "What's going on?" she asked once Clara was back on the line.

"That I can't tell you," Clara said, "but get down here."

There was no coincidence with God.

If Zach hadn't been there on this day and at

that time, August could have died. Alone. Zach marveled at how God had watched out for August.

Like He did for the sparrow.

Like He hadn't done for Sandy.

A ruptured appendix.

Zach had managed to keep August from falling and brought him gently to the floor. Realizing he had left his cell in the car, Zach had rushed back to August's desk to call 9-1-1.

Just before they took him back for surgery, the other man had clung to Zach, sweating and huffing when he asked Zach to take care of the church. Of course, he had said yes, all the while questioning why God would save one person but not another.

Sitting in the waiting area of the hospital's surgical wing, Zach eyed the clock. He had been there for hours. It was close to 11:30 p.m. Mia must be asleep by now. His gut churned, picturing his daughter crying or upset because she hadn't heard from him.

He had been so concerned about August that he'd jumped into the ambulance instead of driving his truck. He hadn't thought to grab his phone until the receptionist had come looking for him, saying Kelsey had called. The first thing he was going to do when he left here was memorize her phone number.

"Zach!" a voice he knew called out.

He swung around and spotted the anxious faces of Kelsey and Sienna. Kelsey rushed over to him. He could see her hesitation and knew what she wanted to do. He opened his arms and pulled both women close.

"Is Pastor Reid okay?" Sienna asked.

He released them and nodded. "Yes. His appendix burst. But he got here in time and made it out of surgery without a problem. I'm just waiting for him to come out of recovery. The nurse said they were working on getting him a room."

Kelsey rested a hand on his arm.

"I'm so glad you were there, or we all could have been crying right now," Sienna said. "I'm going to go see if I can get any news about the pastor. He's going to want me to contact Deacon Rose."

Kelsey nodded, but her attention was fixed on Zach. Her chin wobbled as she looked him square in the face. "I'm so glad you're okay. I don't know what I would've done if something happened to you. What Mia would've…" She broke off, her voice cracking.

Zach stood, humbled at the raw emotion on her face. His arms yearned to cradle her against his chest, and he loved how she wasn't shy to express her feelings. "Was Mia asking for me?"

They headed to sit in two chairs near the entrance of the room.

"You know it. By the way, in case you're wondering, Jade and Izzy are with the girls," she said, chortling through her tears. She sat next to him while she elaborated. "She wanted to show off her outfits, so get ready for the fashion show when you see her next."

He chuckled. She joined him, tapping his arm. Whenever they made contact, there was a buzz, an electrical pulse that crackled to life. He didn't want to delve too deep into why it happened—he could only admit that it did.

"I can't wait to see her new clothes. Thank you so much for taking her with you and Morgan."

Kelsey waved a hand. "It's no problem. As a matter of fact, I'm the one who should be thanking you. Having Mia with us made shopping a much more pleasant experience. Morgan didn't fuss about buying new clothes—which she desperately needed. In fact, she was the main one picking up shirts and shorts, trying to find two sets of everything."

He noticed she had a bag in her hand. She must have seen him look, because she picked up the Wawa bag, held it out and said, "I wasn't sure if you had eaten, so I brought you some chicken noodle soup and a turkey sandwich."

"Girl, you're talking my language," Zach said, holding out his hand to accept the food. "Thank you so much for thinking of me." His heart warmed. It was a nice feeling, having someone look out for him.

She lowered her lashes and clasped her hands. He bumped her shoulder lightly and teased, "Don't go getting all shy on me now."

"Don't let it get to your head," she said, giving him a gentle shove in return. "I would have done this for anyone…a stray cat, even."

Zach loved her sense of humor. It felt good joking around with someone—okay, who was he kidding? It felt good joking around with Kelsey with such ease. He enjoyed her company, whether they were making smoothies, talking or just being silent.

He dug into the food, offering her half of the sandwich. After a brief hesitation, she accepted it and took a bite.

Add sharing a meal with her. That felt good. Too good, maybe?

He shrugged. He was too hungry to debate that now. Turning to look at Kelsey, he said in a serious tone, "Kelsey, I know we met under some unusual circumstances, but I want you to know that I appreciate you. I think you're doing an amazing job with Morgan, and I am beginning to consider you more than a coparent of sorts. I see you as a friend, and I think that's important if our children are going to be in each other's lives."

"I'm trying," she said.

"No. You're doing." He finished up his sandwich and placed the wrapper beside the soup on the table next to him and turned toward her. "I know you only see yourself as Morgan's aunt, her caretaker, but you're more than that. You're her parent. God was looking out for Morgan when He gave her you."

Her eyes misted, wetting her lashes. "I'm not sure I deserve that compliment. I don't think I told you that I never intended to be a parent."

"No, you didn't." Zach felt his mouth hang open. He searched her eyes and saw the truth of her words imprinted there. She was actually serious. "Why? If you don't mind my asking."

She shifted her gaze from his and touched her chest. "My mother died in childbirth." Her voice was low with pain. "Giving birth to me. She died because of me." She stared straight ahead. "If it weren't for me, she would be here."

Zach took her hand and steepled their hands together. He liked the feel of her hands in his. Light zaps this time, his mind registered. His heart twisted when he saw the grief painted on her face. He drew in a breath. Kelsey had been walking around with that her entire life. He found himself uttering a quick prayer to God, asking for the right words.

Sliding his tongue across his lips, he said, "Life is not about ifs. Life is about what is. And what is, is that you were meant to be here. That was God's will. His plan. There's no going against it." His words slammed him in the gut and sliced him in the heart. Those words were for his benefit as much as hers. Judging by her pursed lips, Zach would say Kelsey didn't believe him. He wiped his brow. "You're a parent. I want you to take a moment and really think about this question I'm about to ask. If you had to choose between Morgan's life and your own, who would you choose?"

Her hand went to cover her mouth, and her eyes went wide. "Morgan, of course. It only took me this long to answer because I was trying to figure out why you would ask me that. I think that answer is pretty straightforward. I didn't even have to think about it."

"Exactly," he said, slapping his leg. "That's why you're still here and your mother isn't. Both your parents—your earthly and heavenly ones—chose you. You need to accept that."

"You've given me a lot to think about—to pray about." She cocked her head. "I thought you were done with the whole ministry thing." Her eyes were filled with curiosity.

Kelsey's observation pierced his soul.

"I thought so, too." He swallowed. "But this is who I am. I'm seeing that now. There's no running from what God has placed within you to do. I plan on taking baby steps until I find my way back." Zach chucked her under the chin. "Maybe you can help me, friend?"

She nodded. "Maybe we can help each other."

Friendship was a better approach, because distance wasn't practical. Their children made that an impossibility.

"But remember, you do have another Friend," Kelsey felt the need to add.

Zach nodded, but he was more focused on the niggling truth forming in his mind, taking root, growing like ivy on a vine. What would he do about his attraction?

Chapter Eleven

"I hate to tell you, but you've been relegated to the friend zone," Sienna said.

"I agree. And let me tell you, that is not where you want to be," Jade chimed in.

The women stood by the open trunk of Jade's minivan, the scent of smoke in the air. They were supposed to be getting the hot dogs, hamburgers, rolls and condiments while one of the brothers fired up the grill. Instead, they'd taken a moment to catch up, and Kelsey had told them about her conversation with Zach at the hospital.

Kelsey rolled her eyes. "I'm good with friendship," she said, smoothing out her Millennial House of Praise Fourth of July T-shirt, which she wore with white shorts. Sienna had bedazzled her tee with gems, pairing it with jeans, while Jade had cut hers into a tank top with a white tank underneath and a cute flared skirt. Both of her friends looked fierce.

"You expect us to believe that?" Sienna asked. "I saw the way you looked at him just now, checking him out when he walked off with the girls." Zach had grabbed the cooler before announcing that he was going to take the girls to the water slide in the back of the church. Kelsey had dressed them in matching short sets with butterfly wings purchased from the dollar store. Then she had done their hair in buns like Tinker Bell. She and Zach had snapped several pictures of them before driving to the church together. Yes, together. Friends drove to places together.

Kelsey knew her face went red. "I wasn't 'checking him out,'" she said, using her hands to form air quotes. "If I was looking, it was because this is the first time he's wearing everyday clothes like shorts and sneakers." And he was looking fine. She dipped into the trunk to get the cardboard box holding the ketchup, mustard and relish. Jade clicked the button on her key fob to close the trunk. Kelsey made sure to move out of the way so it wouldn't hit her on the head.

"He knows how to put himself together. I've got to give him that," Jade said with a glint in her eye.

Kelsey gave her friend the side-eye. "Are you

crushing on him?" She felt a peculiar whirl in her stomach and touched her abdomen.

Jade picked up the bags of hot dogs and hamburgers. "Just making an observation." She cracked up, jabbing Kelsey in the elbow. "Naw, girl. I wanted to see if you'd get jealous."

Sienna giggled, grabbing the rolls. "You know you wrong for that, right?"

"Whatever." Kelsey wouldn't admit how she felt lighter hearing her friend jested. They had never shared the same taste in men before. Not that she was interested in Zach.

"Easy, lady. We know that's yours." Sienna wagged her brows.

"He's not mine," Kelsey said as they began to make their way across the parking lot. "He's my friend. That's all." A friend she cared about. A friend she'd spent the past few evenings talking to after the girls were asleep. A friend she had plans to bake an apple pie with—though she couldn't bake, so she would purchase one from the Amish—because he said it was his favorite.

"Well, your *friend* is fine," Jade snickered.

Kelsey gave her a look of irritation. "Looks aren't everything. They fade. I'm interested in his character and how he treats Morgan. He's great with her—and patient. That's what I appreciate." There was that funny feeling again, swirling up her gut, which she ignored. "It is possible for a man and woman to have a platonic friendship," Kelsey pointed out.

"Listen, it's possible for me to eat an entire pizza. It doesn't mean I'm going to do it," Sienna replied. "That's the way I feel about that whole platonic thing. It's possible, but I'm not doing the whole friendship thing with men. I have you two for that. If you see me all chummy with a man, that's because we're dating."

"What man?" Jade said. "We haven't seen you with anybody." Her chunky earrings swayed with her movement.

"Exactly. Because I'm not dating." Sienna ran her fingers through her braids. "I'm going from hello to honeymoon once God points out the one He has for me."

Kelsey snorted. "Girl, you're a trip. You had me going there for a minute."

All of a sudden, Sienna stopped and arched a brow. "Be ready, girl," she said in a low tone.

Jade's mouth dropped open. "Whoa. They have your man—er, *friend* surrounded."

Furrowing her brows, Kelsey followed the direction of her gaze. There had to be about seven—okay, three—women circling around Zach. She had no idea where the girls were. She bit her inner cheeks to keep from grunting. Then she marched forward with her friends flanking her.

"You know it's because of Zach's sermon," Jade said under her breath when they drew close. Zach had announced that he would be taking over while August recovered. Then he had preached on God's grace, providing a lot of Scriptures. Kelsey had taken a lot of notes and had been moved to see him walk in his gift. To say Zach was called would be an understatement.

"No. I think it's because Joel had to take his picture and make it front-page news, calling him Swallow's Creek's most eligible bachelor," Sienna added. "He even posted it on the Swallow's Creek Facebook page."

Kelsey paused and took several deep breaths to calm herself. She remembered seeing the article in the paper. She had vacillated between wanting to cut out and frame Zach's picture to rolling up the newspaper and bopping Joel on the head. Sienna and Jade chattered on, but she wouldn't be able to recall anything, because her eyes were peeled for Zach. And those women. Squawking around him like hens around corn. They were so obvious. Zach had a small smile on his face, like he enjoyed the attention. Kelsey forced herself to lift her foot and start moving. Her friends commenced walking. Whatever was whirling inside her had intensified in strength, and it had a bitter taste. Maybe she had a bad case of indigestion. Maybe it was the word that began with *J* and ended with *Y.*

Regardless, she squared her shoulders and lifted her chin. She wasn't going to keep gawking. It wasn't like she had any right to feel annoyed at their presence. *Annoyed* was too strong a word. So she made sure to put a bright smile on her face, waving to Zach as she walked by.

There was such a thing as being too polite. He had turned down offers for breakfast, lunch and dinner, but these ladies persisted. Maybe he needed to get a T-shirt with Not Interested printed on it, though he doubted that would stop them.

Zach had been on his way back to assist Kelsey when the sisters approached. They were all talking at once and it was impossible to make conversation, so he had remained quiet and let them chatter. Every inch he stepped, they stepped with him.

Fighting off the claustrophobia, Zach saw Kelsey wave at him. "The girls are with Izzy," he yelled, hoping she would approach. But she only nodded before heading to the back of the church. One of the young women offered him a bite of her corn, with a kernel stuck in her teeth. Zach removed her hand from his arm.

He spotted Deacon Rose and held up a hand.

The deacon bent over laughing. No doubt at him. When he saw Joel, Zach would let him have it for plastering his face all over the paper.

"Ladies, I've got to get going," he said, extricating himself from between them. He had promised August that he would go with Deacon Rose to get the boys. He couldn't go in the correctional facility, but he was going to assist. Zach strode across the lot with a huge amount of relief. He jumped into the passenger side of the church van and released a deep sigh. Then he sent Kelsey a text to let her know his whereabouts. She fired back a thumbs-up emoji, and he slipped his phone into his pocket.

Deacon Rose cackled. "The heat too hot for you, eh?" he asked in his Jamaican accent before turning on the air conditioner. "Don't worry. I gonna cool it down for you."

"Yes, please. I couldn't breathe back there."

"Some women tek your air and some give you life."

The deacon's words gave him goose bumps. He arched a brow at Deacon Rose, seeing the quiet man of short stature in a different light. The deacon appeared to be a man with great perception. Now Zach saw why he was August's right hand.

Zach kept up a steady stream of conversation on the way to the detention center, but the entire time, he thought about that emoji. It felt… impersonal. Just a thumbs-up. No words. He inhaled and admonished himself to stop thinking about that text. That's what friends did. Well, he didn't like it.

This morning when he had awakened, Zach had thought of Sandy. Sorrow had threatened to engulf him under its huge wings. He had lain on his bed with one leg on and one leg off, tempted to mope around the house. Then Kelsey had called, brightening his day with talk of getting the girls ready. Her enthusiasm was the antidote to his sadness. He had gotten Mia up, and they had walked to Kelsey's house. Seeing her sparkling eyes and excitement gave him the energy to face the day. Yet, now, she had given him a thumbs-up.

His chest constricted. He needed Kelsey to get through today.

Deacon Rose pulled the van into the visitor parking lot. "I'll be back in a few," he said, leaving Zach with his thoughts. He pulled his phone out of his pocket and looked at that emoji, shaking his head.

Just then, Kelsey's words came back to him. *You do have another Friend.*

Since the day in the hospital, Zach hadn't prayed. Hadn't reached out to God. "I don't have the words," he said aloud.

Zach looked at his watch. It was close to 12:56 p.m. Four hours and four minutes until the exact anniversary of his wife's death. Her last breath. He rolled down the window, even though he would let out some of the cool air. He needed fresh air. This was his first year not visiting Sandy's grave. He should have driven to Philadelphia. Zach didn't understand what he was doing here.

Then the deacon returned with seven young men trailing behind them. These boys had been screened and were not a flight risk. There were two guards accompanying them, dressed in regular garb. The youth had on street clothes, looking like any other young men, only they wore handcuffs.

They were why he was here.

The hard truth was, they were alive, and Sandy wasn't. A fact that made his lungs tighten, but a fact nonetheless.

He couldn't help her. He could help them. A frisson of fear fluttered in his rib cage. They were young, but they had been convicted of crimes. Some serious. August's words comforted him. *Everybody needs a second chance sometimes.* He rebuked his fear, relaxed and jumped out to open the door for them.

What Zach saw on their faces when they approached was uncertainty. Nervousness. In a flash, he realized they weren't certain how he would react to them. If he would accept them without judgment. Zach greeted every young man, looking them in their eyes, making a connection.

Each one answered with, "Nice to meet you, sir."

Once everyone was settled, Zach prayed on the inside, *God, help me to help them.* Then he twisted his body and asked, "So, tell me, what do you know about basketball?"

Chapter Twelve

Spectators stood on the left and the competitors gathered in the middle to await Sienna's instructions. Her friend had set up the table, displaying the four trophies—two for the adults and two for the children—and ribbons. To win the trophy, you needed to win the egg race, the potato sack race and the three-legged race.

Kelsey rubbed her hands together after completing her squats to warm up. She was taking home that trophy, intending to place it on the mantle next to last year's trophy. Though this year, she would have a new partner.

Last year, Jade and Clara had come close to winning the egg race, but Jade had dropped the egg just before the finish line. The year before Jade had tripped on her shoelace and had dropped the egg as soon as it started. But despite those mishaps, Jade was Kelsey's best bet to win. Jade had purchased no-lace sneakers and had promised to powder her hands.

If Kelsey had her way, it would be a double win for her household.

First up were the twins. "Are you girls ready?" Kelsey said, taking off their butterfly wings. Two heads bobbed. She took a moment to adjust Mia's hair, which had come undone, and pulled a baby wipe from her cross-body bag—she had learned not to be without one—and wiped at the ketchup stain on the child's chest. She shook her head, hiding a grin. She didn't know how Mia managed to look so scruffy. Morgan had dirt streaked across her forehead, which she wiped away, but she looked almost the same as when they had arrived.

Mia jumped up and down. "We're gonna win."

"That's the spirit." Kelsey lifted a hand to Morgan for a high five.

Morgan slapped her hand and gave a bright smile. "We got this," she said, doing a little jig.

Ever since the therapy visit, Kelsey had made sure to keep up a positive attitude around her niece. No more crying in the mornings—at least not that Morgan could see. Instead, she treated each day with the brightness of the morning sun, in essence, giving Morgan permission to do the same.

She could see the effect it had already on her niece, and it had only been a week or so. The change lifted her soul. It was jarring to know how much the adults in a child's life contributed to their beliefs, attitude and behaviors. Kelsey was determined for Morgan to triumph past her tragedy, and it began with Kelsey. The weight of that responsibility would have curved her shoulders, but having Zach and Mia in their lives helped to keep her standing. She watched how Zach interacted with Mia and did the same.

Zach had been playing basketball with the boys from the juvenile center for over an hour, but he had promised to come watch the races. Sure enough, she could spot him heading their way.

"Come, Daddy," Mia yelled. "We're about to race."

Zach lifted a hand before jogging over to where they stood. He bent and scooped the girls under his long arms, giving them a squeeze. "I'm here. I wouldn't miss this for anything. I can't wait to watch you. Try your best, but remember it's all about having fun out there today."

Bump that. Her girls were getting that trophy. Kelsey gathered them for a pep talk. "Now listen, there are four other teams, and you have to watch out for the Lewis tribe, but keep your eyes on the egg and the finish line and you'll be okay."

Mia lifted her chin. "We can't drop the egg?"

"No. You can't touch it, either," Kelsey reminded her, squeezing her cheek.

"I won't drop it," Morgan promised with a solemn face. *Oh, my.* She had done it again. Kelsey didn't want her niece believing she would be mad if she didn't win.

Touching Morgan's chin, Kelsey met Zach's eyes. He arched a brow, wordlessly urging her to help Morgan relax. "Just have fun, honey." She forced the words out, but on the inside, she was screaming, *I want you to win.* She was rewarded when Morgan's face relaxed into a smile.

"Are you playing, Ms. Kelsey?" Mia asked.

Kelsey nodded. "I'll be doing the same races you do with the adults."

"If you're competing in the children's egg race, meet me over here so I can go over the rules," Sienna said.

Mia and Morgan skipped over to where she stood. They had a bigger spoon for the younger children to use. She watched them take their places. "Let's go cheer them on," she said, tugging Zach's hand. She meandered her way to the front of the crowd waiting at the finish line.

Zach came over to whisper in her ear. "I didn't know you were so competitive."

Her insides shivered. "I am. I am," she said, before cocking her head. "You played basketball. Didn't you play to win?"

"Yes, but it was about more than winning. It's also about sportsmanship. Teamwork."

She rolled her eyes. "But it's sweet to win."

Jade ran over to where Kelsey stood.

"Where have you been? We have to warm up," Kelsey said, jogging in place. "I already did my squats. Catch up so we can stretch."

"I won't be able to be your partner. Sienna needs me to help with judging. One of the judges had to drop out. Upset stomach." Her friend twisted her hands, refusing to meet her eyes.

She couldn't be mad at someone getting sick. "Can't she find someone else?" she asked, her eyes scanning the crowd to see who needed a partner. Or rather, who she thought could win that needed a partner.

Jade rubbed Kelsey on the back. "There's always next year. I'm sorry, honey. But maybe this is good. You're not a gracious loser."

Disappointment slashed her gut, hunching her back. "I'm trying to keep my family's legacy going." Kennedy and Kelsey had been the champs since they were fourteen. "It's just that it's important to me. It's one way I can honor Kennedy."

Jade's eyes held sympathy. "I get it. I understand." Cocking her head toward the girls, she said, "Root for Morgan and Mia. It might be time to pass the mantle."

Sienna blew the whistle, and Jade took off to join the other judges. Kelsey swallowed and wiped at her eyes as the familiar sadness built around her. It was a good thing Morgan wasn't near or she'd be feeding off Kelsey's despondency.

Speaking of Morgan, Kelsey gave herself a mental shake and pushed past her sorrow to cheer on her niece and Mia.

Zach had seen basketball with the boys as duty. An unselfish act. Ministry. That's why he had been able to face this day. But when he overheard Kelsey and Jade's conversation, Zach knew if he volunteered, it would be about putting a smile on Kelsey's face. On the day his wife had died.

Zach tried to ignore the effects of Kelsey's disappointment. He tried to squelch the desire to be her person, but it was building like ants on sugar. He fought against his mind, raging at him to step in, be her hero. He had heard her mention honoring her sister, however, he would be dishonoring his wife if he helped her. In his heart, he knew that Sandy wouldn't want him to remain wrapped in a cocoon of grief. She had encouraged him to move on. But he couldn't. To move on would mean Sandy hadn't mattered.

Still, he found himself inching closer to Kelsey. He could see the grief on her face, her brave attempt to cheer the girls on. His heart screamed at him to put a smile on her face. Zach fought with himself right up until his mouth betrayed him.

"I'll do it," he huffed out.

She furrowed her brows. "Do what?" she asked, before cupping her mouth and yelling, "That's it, Morgan, run to Mia. Run to Mia." When Morgan made it without dropping the egg, Kelsey twirled. "That's my girl. That's my girl." This was the first time Zach had heard her refer to Morgan as her own—in a roundabout way. Next it was Mia's turn. Kelsey showed the same enthusiasm for his daughter.

That sealed his decision to participate. He draped an arm around her shoulders and said, "I am going to be your partner in the race." Then he pulled his arm away, shocked at how right that had felt.

"Thank you." Her eyes showed her true elation, although her response was more subdued.

Zach watched Mia's stubby legs move swiftly across the field and rooted her on. There was a moment when she almost collided with a little girl next to her. He found himself grabbing Kelsey's hand. Her other hand was over her mouth. But his baby straightened her path and shot past the finish line. In first place. When he heard her and Morgan's names announced as the winners, his chest puffed, and he pumped his fists in the air. All for an egg race.

He and Kelsey hugged and ran over to where the girls stood.

"You guys were amazing," Kelsey said.

They nodded.

"We're the best," Mia said, then beckoned to Morgan, who came to join her.

Their cheeks were flushed and their chests heaved, but Zach could see the joy on their faces at their triumph. He scooped them up and swung them around before they wiggled out of his arms.

"We won," Morgan said, jumping up and down. "I want to do another one."

From the corner of his eye, he could see Kelsey's eyes go wide. Zach wanted to cheer Morgan for talking up but figured it was best to act like it was no big deal. His hand moved of its own will to grasp on to Kelsey's and give it a tight squeeze. She nodded in return. He liked how they could communicate without saying a word.

Just like he had with Sandy.

His smile dimmed like a cloud covering the sun. Guilt slashed his being. He retreated a step but Kelsey crooked her finger at him.

"It's our turn," she said.

Zach lagged behind her as they stopped to leave the girls under Izzy's care. The urge to back out built like bile in his stomach, and he had to clench his jaw to keep from vomiting the words that would squash Kelsey's expectations.

Her eyes narrowed. "Are you okay?" she asked.

His body rocked with indecision. Then, ignoring the dueling battles within him of wanting to please Kelsey versus sinking into the despair of losing his wife on this day, Zach took a step forward. And onto the field.

Chapter Thirteen

"Woot! Woot! We did it," Kelsey said, waving the trophy in the air. "Sis, this one's for you, and it will hold a special place on your mantel." She stood by the judging table, where she had just collected her prize for winning all the events. All thanks to Zach.

He had stopped a few feet away to tie his shoelaces, with Morgan and Mia climbing all over his back. The girls' trophy rested by his feet. His jubilation had been a lot more reserved, but Kelsey enjoyed his competitive spirit and his long legs.

He stood, hoisting both girls in his arms, his muscles bulging under the effort, and gave her a weary smile. Going over to extricate the girls from his arms and pick up the trophy off the ground, Kelsey said, "You must be exhausted. Thank you so much for doing this with me. I don't think I can begin to explain how much this meant to me."

"I think I have an idea," he said in a low tone.

"You and Ms. Kelsey made a good team," Mia said, looking between them with a huge grin on her face.

"Yeah. I like that you played together," Morgan said, doing an odd celebratory skip and flapping her arms.

Mia came to stand between them. Tilting her head back, her eyes shone. "There is no *i* in team and two *i*'s make an us," she said, pointing her hand between them. Kelsey chuckled. Zach must have taught her that.

"I guess," Kelsey said with a lopsided grin before making eye contact with Zach above their heads. He scrunched his lips together, his look one of resignation. Her eyes narrowed. What was going on here?

"I'll tell you later," he mouthed.

Morgan squeezed her way between them to join her sister. Taking Mia's hand, she breathed out. "I like us together. It's us and them." She gave Mia a grave look, and Mia bobbed her head like she was pleased with her sister's words.

Kelsey could only shake her head, not sure who the "them" was, but she shrugged, deciding not to try to understand the logic of five-year-olds. Instead, she ruffled their hair and said, "I think we all deserve milkshakes at the MacGrady's stand."

"Yay!" both girls yelled and took off to join the line a few feet away.

Zach rubbed between his eyes. "If it's all right with you, can I call a rain check?"

She nodded, feeling let down and not sure she wanted to examine why. "Sure. You look exhausted. Why don't you head home and rest? I can keep Mia, and we can all hitch a ride with Sienna."

The fact that he didn't argue increased her concern. He simply said, "That sounds good," and chucked her on the chin. "Take care of your trophy."

"Are you okay?"

He shrugged. "I just need…" He cleared his throat. "I've got to get home."

Kelsey wanted to ask him outright what was wrong. To urge him to talk to her. But friends didn't push. She sensed that whatever was going on with him, Zach really wanted to be alone. So, despite her heart screaming for her to persist, Kelsey patted his arm and gave the expected response of "I'm here if you need me" before letting him go.

He stuffed his hands in his shorts pockets and walked away, his shoulders drooping. Kelsey chewed on her lower lip, wanting to go after him. The girls were by Sienna, who gave her a wave and a thumbs-up, signaling all was good. Zach was already halfway across the lot. Doubt swirled in her gut. She should run after him and tell him she was concerned, plead with him to talk to her. But she doubted she had the place in his life to do that.

Their friendship was *new* new—still in a fragile, uncertain state. She stretched her neck muscles from side to side. Maybe she was being super sensitive and making more of this than she should. She needed to take his word and let him have his alone time. He had done that for her when she first learned the DNA results. Besides, keeping Mia was her being a friend and helping him.

With her mind settled, Kelsey walked over to join the girls, who were chanting, "We want ice cream," in unison. Joel was behind Sienna and gestured for Kelsey to go in front of him.

"Thank you," she said to him. He nodded, his hands swiping through the screen of his camera as he checked out the pictures he had taken. And he had taken a lot.

"Everything good with Zach?" Sienna asked, her voice filled with concern.

"Yeah…" Kelsey said. "He said he was tired, but he seemed like he had stuff on his mind."

"Of course he had a lot on his mind," Joel said, butting in.

Sienna rolled her eyes. "Does he have to be all up in our business—in our conversation?"

Kelsey placed a hand on her hip and addressed Sienna. "Be nice." Then she centered her focus on Joel, who was now cleaning his camera lens. "What do you mean?"

"Well, contrary to those who think me a pest, I'm a journalist who's respected nationwide," he said, giving Sienna's elbow a light nudge. Kelsey groaned. These two were forever sniping at each other. She twirled her index finger in a circle, gesturing for Joel to continue. "But, anyways, to prepare for my interviews, I do my research."

Sienna whipped her head around. "Will you get to the point? You dragging it out like…like I don't even know what."

Jade and Izzy walked over. "What's going on?"

Joel led them out of the line. For some reason, Kelsey's heart began to thump. "What is it, Joel? Tell me."

Jade, who must have sensed privacy was needed, directed her daughter to take the girls for their ice cream.

He stopped fiddling with his camera, his

voice grave and low. "His wife died two years ago today, on Independence Day."

Sienna gasped, putting a hand on her chest. Kelsey's knees buckled, and she grabbed onto Sienna's arm. Her friend held her against her chest.

"No. That can't be. He was here...playing." She shook her head, trying to process what she had just heard. Trying to picture the man playing basketball, running with her in the egg race and hooting and hollering when the girls won— doing all that when his wife had died on this day. Tears threatened, but she swallowed them down. She looked over at the girls, glad to see they weren't paying her any attention at the moment. She couldn't unravel and have them see. Especially Morgan.

"Are you sure?" she heard Sienna ask through a haze of unbelief forming around her. Kelsey was relieved to hear her friend's voice lacked its usual rancor. She couldn't have taken any bickering between them after what she had just heard.

"Unfortunately, yes. His church in Philadelphia did a big write-up on it and held a memorial service for her."

"How do you know all this?" Jade asked, coming to hold Kelsey up on the other side.

"Google. You'd be surprised at what you can

find." He sauntered off after that with his camera raised, his gaze focused on the twins at the ice cream stand. He had dropped a boulder in her celebration and left her crushed. She was fortunate to have her friends' support.

A sob burst its way to freedom, and she emitted a gurgle and touched her chest. "Oh, my…" She placed a fist in her mouth. "I can't believe this. I am so selfish. I spent most of the day going on about winning these races, getting a trophy, all the while he was grieving his wife. Who does that?" Tears trekked down her face, and her shoulders shook.

"Hush, you didn't know," Jade said as Kelsey cried.

"You had a good reason, too," Sienna reminded her.

She shook her head. That didn't matter. Her victory had come at the expense of his pain. Sienna stalked off and handed tissues to Kelsey when she returned.

"I—I've got to go see him," Kelsey said, mouth dry. She wiped her runny nose and took a step. "I've got to apologize."

"Go ahead," Sienna said. "I'll take the girls. You don't want them to see you falling apart."

"I was going to ride home with you," Kelsey replied.

Jade chimed in, "I'll take you. Let the girls finish their ice cream."

Kelsey broke into fresh tears. "Thank you. I'm so selfish. I don't deserve friends like you. I can't believe I had him out here for hours when he could have been at home."

"Listen, he's a grown man," Sienna said. "Zach doesn't strike me as the type of person who would do something he didn't want to do. So take it easy on yourself. You didn't mean any harm. You were trying to do something for Kennedy. You have your own stuff going on. He's not the only one. Now, if you want to go see him, then go. But quit putting yourself down. I'm going to say a quick prayer for you, but you've got to hold yourself together, girl."

Kelsey wished she could grab onto the comfort provided through Sienna's words, but all she felt for herself was recrimination. Horror. And pain, knowing he was all alone.

Jade scooped her close and began to lead her toward the vehicle. She settled into Jade's minivan and rested her head on the window. Folding her arms about her, she allowed the tears to fall while she prayed. She hated the thought of him being alone.

The pounding on the door along with the doorbell ringing brought Zach out of his stupor. He had arrived home and sunk to the floor in his living room, unable to move. Grief mingled with guilt whipped him like a cat-o'-nine-tails. He had grabbed his head, feeling as if he had chosen wrong. He should have spent this day reflecting on his life with Sandy. Reflecting on what he had lost, not what he could win.

Whoever was at his door was persistent. He held on to the couch and made himself stand. The sudden fear that something could have happened to Mia propelled him to swing the door ajar. He squinted to make out the figure huddled outside his door before he turned on the porch light. Then his mouth dropped open. It was Kelsey, and she looked as if she had been crying.

When he peered around her for the girls, his heart pounded until it echoed in his ears. "What's the matter?" He stepped back, holding the door wider. "Is it Mia? Morgan? Has something happened?"

She pushed her way inside and snaked her arms around his waist.

"What's wrong?" he asked as concern wormed its way from his heart and into his voice, hearing her repeated apologies. "Kelsey, slow down. You are running about five miles ahead of me, and I haven't even taken a step. What's going on?"

"I didn't know it was the anniversary of your wife's passing."

Withholding a gasp, he pulled out of her arms, putting much-needed distance between them, unable to face her. If it weren't for the fact that he didn't want to be rude or hurt her feelings, Zach would have asked her to leave. "Who told you?"

"Joel." She exhaled loud enough for him to hear, though she stood a few feet away.

He clenched his jaw. Joel seemed to be in everybody's business.

Hearing the rustle of her feet, Zach knew she was coming close. Into his personal space. He shook his head, his natural reaction to shut her out. Now that she knew, he felt raw. Exposed. He didn't want to share this emotion with anyone. When she placed a hand on his back, he stiffened.

"You shouldn't be on your own," she said, her voice filled with what sounded like pity.

He lifted his chin. "I'm good." His voice sounded flat and cool, but he couldn't help it. By himself, he had remained stoic, his sorrow a ball in his gut. But her presence made it rise and expand when he needed to keep that ball tight. "Kelsey," he whispered. "You should not have come here. Go home, please." Though deep down, a part of him, the part he would never acknowledge, wanted her to stay.

She circled until she stood in front of him, then tucked her hand under his chin. He dared to look at her from under his lashes.

"I'm not leaving," she said, her voice like steel. Unlike Sandy. Who had left him. He shoved that traitorous thought aside. Sandy had fought the cancer raging through her body long and hard. She tried to stay. In the end, it had been up to God. And Zach had to live with His decision for the rest of his life. Alone.

Grabbing onto him, Kelsey closed her eyes and began praying. The words flowed from her as she poured her heart out to God on his behalf.

Once she was done, Zach thanked her then pushed away, feeling trapped, cornered. "I need you to go. Please."

"I'm not going anywhere." She repeated the words with emphasis. Her eyes, though red, held strength, beckoning him, telling him it was okay to spew out the ball wedged now in his chest.

Zach swung away from her and stormed toward the kitchen. He needed air. He needed space. She followed him. He opened the sliding door and launched himself outside. Taking huge gulps, Zach sank to the earth, his hands fisted on his stomach. He felt Kelsey kneel behind him, her breath raising the hairs on his neck. Zach swallowed the urge to snap at her to leave him alone, even as his back muscles relaxed to be a pillow to her head.

Chapter Fourteen

"This poacher is going to make me either lose my faith or build my prayer life," Kelsey fumed. She paced the small hallway in her office, trying not to howl.

Two clients had called this morning to tell her assistant they were canceling their contracts and signing with Gerald. Two. Another three potentials had avoided her calls.

"You need to pray that man out of that building," Sasha said, fanning herself in the face like it could cool her temper.

"Ugh. I will," Kelsey said. "The commission from the Nguyens' sale has set us ahead—"

"That it did," Sasha interrupted to show off her manicured hands. Kelsey had made sure to give her a bonus once her funds had cleared.

"That commission set us ahead by several months," Kelsey continued, "but we need to build a good cushion, especially if we hope to expand. How long before you're done with your courses?"

She had encouraged Sasha to complete her real estate license. Once she was done, they would be a team of two—partners—and she would hire another assistant.

"I plan on taking the test in the fall. But we have a problem that could interfere with our expansion." Sasha scratched her head. "I have a sneaking suspicion that Gerald has someone posting fake reviews on our webpage, because two one-star reviews popped up trashing us. And I think that's why we're losing people."

He wouldn't.

Of course he would. This was Gerald. Nothing appeared to be out of bounds with him when it came to sabotaging her firm.

"Let me see those," Kelsey said, bending over to read Sasha's screen. What she saw made her eyes bulge, and her mouth dropped open. "They wrote that I was late, unprofessional and rude." She flailed her hands. "That is such hogwash. Who would do this?"

Sasha lifted a brow. "Who you think?"

Heat jumped off her skin like sparks of fire on a Texas road in the middle of summer. Her left eye ticked, and she had to draw steady breaths to keep from exploding. Sasha prodded her with payback suggestions, fueling her ire. She was tempted to storm across the street and confront Gerald, but it wouldn't be the best move.

Isaiah 54:17 came into her mind. *No weapon that is formed against thee shall prosper; and every tongue that shall rise against thee in judgment thou shalt condemn.* She had to repeat that verse a couple more times while her fury abated.

"We will not stoop to his level, no matter how intriguing that notion might be," Kelsey said, massaging her temples. "My good name and work ethic will outshine his dirt. God will handle him."

Sasha looked ready to argue, but she must have seen that Kelsey had made up her mind. Picking up the phone, she said, "Let me make some client calls and fill your calendar."

With a nod, Kelsey strode down the hallway and into her personal office. She had to decompress before putting on her professional mask so she could sell some houses. Kelsey had three houses to show starting at noon, and she couldn't show up agitated. That could ruin a buyer's excitement. Having stayed up until past midnight the night before, after leaving Zach's house, she'd had to put cucumbers on her eyes to reduce their puffiness.

Her cell phone rang, and she fished the phone

out of the pocket of her wide-legged pants. When she saw Zach's name flash across her screen, she moved fast to answer before it went to voice mail.

"Can you stop here when you get a chance?" he asked. His voice sounded scratchy, like gravel underfoot.

"Sure, is everything good?" She touched her bun to assure herself her hair was still as neat as when she had left the house that morning.

"Yes and no. Yes, as in no one has been harmed or in danger. No, because a letter came that you need to see."

She could tell Zach was trying to downplay it, but there was no mistaking the urgency in his tone. Her hands felt sweaty. "I can get there by about two o'clock or so. Do you want me to bring MacGrady's?"

"No, I can make us sandwiches, and I'll have some chicken noodle soup handy."

So, she would need comfort food. She clenched her jaw. Whatever it was, she would have no choice but to face it. But at least this time, she would have Zach by her side. Like chicken soup, he was more than good for her soul.

Kelsey had fussed over him the night before, her nurturing a balm to his bruised heart.

Which was why Zach knew he was going to have to return the favor that afternoon once she got in from work.

He stood by the window in his workroom, looking at the papers he held in his hands, and wiped his brow. It was a scorcher outside, but it was what he held in his hands that had elevated his body temperature.

Zach had just returned from a trip to the mailbox when one particular envelope in the pile of bills caught his eye. The return address was that of a law office. He'd debated whether he should toss it in the trash with other junk mail before he ripped the package open. It was a good thing and a bad thing that he had. When he read the contents, hot anger mixed with panic flared to life.

He was being sued.

His heart twisted. The same summer the girls had found each other, their birth mother, Frances Day, was suing for custody, stating she had rescinded her parental rights under duress.

Releasing a shaky breath, Zach wondered why their mother had decided to do this now. Almost six years had passed since their birth. Mia's adoption had been finalized without a hitch. He had honored her only request by keeping Mia's name. So had Kelsey's sister.

Zach went into the kitchen and laid out the ingredients to make homemade chicken soup. He would prepare it and then rewarm it once Kelsey arrived. He made a quick trip to the supermarket to buy sandwich meat, fresh romaine lettuce and tomatoes. Once he returned, Zach put the water on to boil along with thyme and bouillon cubes. He washed the chicken breast, whistling as he worked before slicing it into chunks and putting it in the pot. The aroma from the kitchen made his stomach growl. Next, he chopped up the carrots and celery. When Kelsey texted that she was on her way not even forty minutes after he had spoken to her, Zach rushed to finish adding the other ingredients.

The doorbell rang just as he was about to make the sandwiches.

Kelsey came in and gave him a brief hug before making her way into the kitchen. She rested her satchel on top of the island and took one of the seats.

Sniffing the air, she patted her stomach with appreciation. "It smells like some home cooking in here."

Zach used one of the towels hanging on his oven door to wipe his hands. "I thought you weren't coming until about two?" He said the last word as a question and reached into the cupboard to take out two plates and a bowl. Then he stood across from her so they could talk while he made their sandwiches. Kelsey volunteered to help, but he didn't need it.

"Yes, but my clients called and said something popped up." Her shoulders curved, and he could hear the worry in her tone. "I don't think it's something but rather someone. Remember, I told you about Gerald? Somehow he is getting my clients' information and talking them into signing with him."

"I would think there would be more than enough to go around."

She slapped a hand on the table. "They aren't the first ones, either. On top of it, he's defaming my character on review sites. All this because I refused to sign with him. But it is precisely because of this kind of behavior that I know I made the right decision."

Zach inclined his head. "Isn't there a governing board you could report him to? These actions should get his real estate license revoked."

"How would I prove it? All I have to go on is a hunch. The clients are free to sign with whomever they choose. Even though we both signed a contract, I can't stop them from deciding to leave. I wouldn't do that anyway if I could."

He wasn't surprised. That spoke a lot about her character. "People like that never prosper for long," he said. "He's going to experience a rude awakening. For a hundred years, Noah endured the ridicule of those around him who had never seen rain and who insisted on living outside God's will. But when the thunder came and the waters began to come down in a downpour, not even Noah could open the door to save them." He stirred the soup and turned the heat down to a low simmer.

"I hope it doesn't take a hundred years," she said in a teasing tone.

"It will happen at the right time. God moves in His time, and all nature bows to His plan."

She waved a hand, "Look at you, preaching and stuff, giving me some good spiritual advice, Mr. I'm Not a Minister Anymore."

He chuckled. "Like I said, all nature bows to His plan, eventually."

They ate their meal side by side and, despite her situation, managed to share a few laughs. It felt good being able to spend time as friends. He enjoyed her company and her sense of humor. Once they were finished and he had placed their plates and silverware in the dishwasher, Zach knew it was time to stop stalling.

"I hate to add to your distress, but we have a serious situation on our hands that we will have to face together."

He watched her eyes widen. "If I hadn't already eaten, I would have lost my appetite at those words." She rested a hand on his arm.

"What is it? Tell me. And what business could we have together besides the girls?"

"A letter came today from the law firm of Weidner and Weidner. The girls' birth mother wants to revoke the adoption. She is seeking custody of the girls. I suspect you probably have a similar letter waiting for you at home, or on the way to you."

Kelsey gripped the edge of the bar. He reached out a hand to steady her or she might have fallen. She whirled on him. "Why did you wait almost an hour to tell me something like this?"

"Because if I told you, you wouldn't have eaten, and you needed to vent." Zach gestured for her to follow him into his workspace.

"That could have all waited. This was more important," she shot back, traipsing behind him. "I get that we're doing the whole being-there-for-each-other thing, but anything involving Morgan is a priority. I would think it would be the same for you with Mia."

"You're right," Zach said. "I shouldn't have made that decision for you."

"That's okay. I know you meant well. No use complaining over already-eaten soup." Her displeasure evaporated at the speed of a cheap firecracker.

He chuckled at her rephrasing of the spilled milk expression. Her eyes scanned the room, taking in a model car on his desk along with the others he had completed.

Picking up the letter, he handed it to her to read, clasping his hands in front of him as he observed Kelsey's rapid eye movements and her furrowed brows. Zach could tell the exact moment she arrived at *that* part. She placed a hand over her mouth and looked like she was about to be sick.

Then she shook her head. "No. This can't be right. This can't be happening." Her voice rose. "This is beginning to feel like the longest day of my life. Please, tell me this is not happening."

"I wish I could. This is the beginning of every adoptive parent's nightmare."

She massaged between her eyes. "I can't take any more shocks to my system today. I can't. My sister trusted me to take care of Morgan. I can't disappoint her, and I can't bear to lose Morgan."

Zach flashed back to Sandy's final days. She had grabbed his arm and made him promise to take care of their little girl. He had kept his word. Now, this lawsuit threatened to annihilate that promise. Zach wouldn't allow that to happen.

Mia was his daughter.

His and Sandy's.

He wouldn't give her up without a serious

fight. This time he reached for Kelsey's hand without any second-guessing. Her smaller hand trembled under his.

Giving it a light squeeze, Zach reassured her, "I don't know about you, but I'm not handing my daughter over to a stranger. I'm going to get an attorney, and I think we should join forces, put our resources together and fight this."

"I agree." Her voice wobbled, but her eyes held resolve. She drew in a deep breath and nodded. "I think I know just the right person to defend us."

"I hate to sound like a snobby outsider, but I think I need to hire someone outside this small town."

"You don't know Trent West like I do. He's a bulldog and the best in town. Make that the state. If anyone can win this case, he can."

Her confidence in this Trent West made up Zach's mind. "All right. Let's see if he's available and get him on retainer."

"I'll give him a call. Then I was thinking of asking Joel to find out what he can about Frances Day."

Zach nodded.

She secured an appointment with the attorney and contacted Joel, then left to return to work. Zach stalked to the calendar on his refrigerator and penciled in his appointment with Trent West, writing in the words *lawsuit* and *custody*.

This was the time to get on his knees and ask God's guidance. However his trust in Him was still shaken. In this case, Zach would rely on the letter of the law. Because unlike with God, there was always a loophole if things didn't go his way.

Losing Sandy had shattered him. He couldn't lose Mia. If he did, he might never recover.

Chapter Fifteen

The deejay Pastor Reid had hired had the children gyrating their little bodies to the beat. The camp's main room had been cleared out to make room for dancing, and there were balloons and streamers and photos posted of the counselors and all the children in the camp. Kelsey had already found Mia's and Morgan's and would snatch them up at the end of the night.

There were two huge tables in the center of the room, laden with hot dogs, potato chips, popcorn and cupcakes. In one corner of the room, children were lined up to get their faces painted. In another, some waited to get cotton candy. Among them were Mia and Morgan, each holding one of Zach's hands. She squinted, noticing that Mia's tiara was bent to the side. She shook her head and grinned.

She and Zach had debated whether to come

after learning of the custody battle. However, as Zach pointed out, their appointment with Trent had been set for the following week. There was no point staying at home dwelling on what could happen, thus keeping the girls from enjoying themselves. She had agreed. Her rationale was it was better to keep creating good memories… just in case.

"You outdid yourself this year," Kelsey shouted to Sienna so she could be heard above the music.

"I try," Sienna said, batting her lashes. Then she grew serious. "You know every year I say it's my last time, but when it comes down to it, I do this for the children. The joy on their faces makes all I do worthwhile."

Kelsey agreed. Mia and Morgan had spoken about nothing else these past days. Pointing toward the far end of the room, she observed, "Jade's photo booth is a success." Her line was the longest.

"Chile, when she told me she wanted to purchase costumes so the children could become beloved African American heroes, I just knew it was going to be a blip. But it's a hit."

Children and parents were waiting to pose as Harriet Tubman, Malcolm X, Sojourner Truth and others.

"Combining fashion with history creates an

appreciation for the struggles of those in the past. It's sheer genius. We're definitely going to have to do that again next year," Sienna said.

"So you're already committing," Kelsey replied with a hand on her hip.

"I guess. Might as well accept what I cannot change."

The deejay switched the tune, and Sienna started doing some old-school moves. Kelsey jumped in to join her before Sienna shimmied away to keep a little girl from dipping her finger in the punch. Zach returned to her side, each of the girls holding cotton candy, one pink, one blue.

"This is yummy," Mia said, sticking out her tongue to taste the treat. Mia had pieces in her hair, and her dress had a tear.

Zach must have followed the direction of her eyes, because he said, "Trust me, I have been trying to figure out how that happens. Take my advice and quit trying."

"Yes. I like cotton candy," Morgan said, biting into the huge puff. Some got on her nose. "It's sticky."

"Yes, it is." Kelsey chuckled before removing it with her thumb. "There you go."

"Thanks, Mom," Morgan said, then continued eating her cotton candy like she hadn't shifted Kelsey's paradigm.

Kelsey swayed, then gasped. Morgan must have made a mistake. She wasn't... She shook her head, unsure of how to feel about her niece calling her Mom. That was reserved for Kennedy. She looked at Zach with wide eyes. He placed a finger over her lips, his multicolored eyes begging her not to react.

Before she could recover, Izzy came over. "My mom wants the girls to pose for a picture," the teen said, sporting a painted unicorn on her face.

"Okay, I'll bring them after they've washed their hands," Kelsey said.

The deejay announced he was about to slow things down. "This one's for the parents. Grab a partner's hand and come to the middle of the floor." She watched as couples shuffled to the floor at their children's bidding—some looked delighted, and others wore slightly uncomfortable grins.

"Daddy, you need to take Ms. Kelsey," Mia said in a loud voice. "They are asking for parents. And you're parents."

"Yes, it's your turn," Morgan said, pulling her at the waist.

"I don't think Ms. Kelsey wants to dance," Zach said.

"She likes to dance," Morgan said, tugging Kelsey's hand.

"I can take them to wash their hands if you want," Izzy piped up, trying to be helpful.

Kelsey stood rooted, knowing her face was flushed. The girls were being insistent about them going on the dance floor together. Dancing meant getting close, touching shoulders or lower backs. They were friends, but there was no need for them to get that…friendly. It wasn't like she hadn't touched him or hugged him—Kelsey had done plenty of that, especially over the past few days. But she'd had a reason then. Their physical interactions had been about comfort. Not… pleasure. Not to say it didn't feel good having his strong arms wrapped around her and inhaling his masculine scent.

Then she spotted two women heading toward them with determined faces. She had noticed them trying to engage Zach in conversation, openly flirting while she stood there—as if she didn't matter.

Snatching Zach's hand, she said to Izzy, "We'll come find you when we're done," and led Zach to the dance floor. To say she was satisfied at the gaping women with jealousy all over their faces was an understatement.

Zach chuckled and drew her close. They began to sway to the music. "I saw what you did, but thanks for the rescue."

She settled into his arms. "You're welcome. I

didn't think you wanted the crane and the flamingo pecking around you anymore tonight." He was a good dancer. She probably would have enjoyed it more if she didn't feel he was doing it out of obligation—or because she'd dragged him onto the dance floor.

He tilted his head and laughed, his shoulders shaking against her chest. "I can't believe you compared them to birds."

"Long-necked birds," she corrected. Then tapped his shoulder. "So, is it my imagination or were the girls determined that we dance together?"

"No, they were trying to do that. Mia wants us to be together."

She shivered from his voice in her ear. She was enjoying this a bit too much. "I think it's all about her and Morgan being together."

Zach chuckled. "Of course. What else could it be?"

She snorted, pretending her heart rate hadn't increased because he'd closed the distance between them. She had no answer to that question, so she broached the concern uppermost in her mind. "What do I do about Morgan calling me Mom?" she whispered.

"Let her," he said, leading her across the floor. The deejay slipped into another slow jam.

She pushed against his chest, all the while

keeping up with his rhythm. "But what about Kennedy?" Kelsey couldn't begin to articulate the guilt she felt at replacing Kennedy in Morgan's heart.

"Morgan is five years old," he pointed out in a gentle tone. "For her, six months is a lifetime. She's a happy child. Right now, you're taking care of her. You're her constant. You're her person. She knows she can rely on you. You are her mom. It's time you accept that. I don't think she's forgotten who Kennedy is, but she wants to acknowledge who you are to her."

His words made sense. "You gave me something to think about. It just feels too soon." She lifted her chin. "What would you do if Mia called someone else Mom?"

Zach missed his step. "There's no chance of that happening." The music was about to end, and he twirled her around before dipping her low.

Her chest heaved. She wasn't sure if it was from his bold dance move or from the words he had just uttered. "No chance?" she dared to ask.

"None. I have no intentions of replacing her mom."

She nodded, but Kelsey pondered his words. Mainly, why had her heart squeezed at hearing Zach basically say his wife was irreplaceable? Why did that leave her feeling hollow inside?

* * *

It was the Sunday evening after the dance, and Zach and Kelsey had decided to meet at her home. Joel was coming by to share the information he had gathered on Frances Day.

"Mia!" he called up the stairs. "Are you ready to go?"

She plunked down the stairs dressed in her Elsa outfit and rain boots. Zach put a hand on her shoulder. "You can't wear that."

"But it's raining outside," Mia said, pouting.

"Yes, but your Elsa outfit is too big for you."

Mia stomped her feet and broke into tears. "I want to wear it."

Zach twisted her around until she faced the bottom of the stairs. "Get upstairs and put on the clothes I laid out for you to wear."

She dug her feet in and folded her arms. His brows rose. Zach knew she wasn't about to act out when it was time to leave. He wasn't going to have this little girl embarrass him out in public—or in his home. "This is my last warning. I shouldn't have to repeat myself. Am I going to have to put you into time-out?"

"Morgan's wearing her Elsa outfit." Her shoulders shook as she broke into a crying fest. Zach inhaled and told himself not to lose patience. He wished this was the only problem he had. She was worried about an outfit. He was worried about losing her. If only his life was that simple.

"Get upstairs, now," he directed in a firm tone.

She stomped up the stairs and returned a few minutes later dressed in the shorts and tee. Her mouth was twisted into a pout.

"We have to go because I don't want to be late, but when we get to Ms. Kelsey's house, you're in time-out. You hear me?"

Her little head bobbed. On the outside he kept his facial expression stern, but, on the inside, his heart melted. He hated to see the distress on Mia's face, but she had to learn to follow his directions. Zach grabbed some tissues and wiped her eyes and nose. "Do you have your iPad?"

She shook her head. "Morgan and I are playing house. I won't need it."

Zach guided her through the door, and they walked up the block. His daughter sulked the entire way, her usual chatter nonexistent. He shrugged. She would get over it, because he wasn't going to back down.

They arrived at Kelsey's house, and he rang the doorbell. When Kelsey opened the door, she took in Mia's poked-out lips and gave him a look of understanding. Mia moved toward the staircase, but Zach reminded her she would be in time-out. She broke into another round of tears.

"Let me guess—the Elsa outfit?" Kelsey asked, raising her voice above Mia's wailing. Kelsey had on a pair of jeans, and her head was wrapped with a head scarf. He knew from being married to Sandy that meant she was in cleaning mode.

His brow arched. "Yep."

"We had the same situation here. Morgan is upstairs changing." She flailed her hands and laughed. "I don't know what we're going to do when they become teenagers. I think we have divas in the making." Then she sobered, saying under her breath, "If they are still with us."

"They will be," Zach said. "We'll pay good money to make sure they stay with us."

Kelsey excused herself and went toward the kitchen.

He walked into her living room and saw that she had dusted and vacuumed and the room smelled of lavender. Zach led a wooden Mia to stand in the corner. Then he set his watch for five minutes and sat on Kelsey's couch, determined to ignore his daughter, who was sniffling quietly while her shoulders shook. Zach had to look away to keep from caving. This was going to be a long five minutes. He rarely had to discipline Mia, and it was the part of parenting he hated the most, but it had to be done.

Kelsey returned with a tray that had a pitcher of lemonade and three glasses. She jerked her head in Mia's direction, her eyes full of sympathy. "How much longer?"

He exhaled. "Four minutes."

"Let me freshen up the bathroom," Kelsey said and dipped into the half bath.

Morgan came downstairs wearing a sundress. When she saw her sister in the corner, her chin quivered, and a tear rolled down her face. Great. Now they had two girls crying. Morgan went over to where her sister stood and held her hand. Mia rested her head against Morgan's. He swallowed, his heart breaking at that show of solidarity. He probably should have told Morgan to let Mia serve her time alone, but he couldn't. He just couldn't.

Kelsey popped out of the bathroom, wiping her hands on a paper towel. She had taken off her scarf and donned a headband. When she saw the girls standing together, she cupped her mouth before dabbing at her eyes. Really? Kelsey sat next to him, her hands folded in her lap. He ignored Kelsey's pleading eyes, silently begging for this to be over.

"I see how this is," Zach said, looking at his

timer. He was on his own. One minute. One glorious minute and this would be over.

Finally. The buzz invaded the quiet. And the air lightened.

Mia came out of the corner and gave him a hug. "I'm sorry, Daddy." Morgan huddled close.

"Next time Daddy tells you to do something, you have to listen, okay, baby girl?" When she nodded, he patted her on the back and said, "Okay, go play with your sister."

Morgan gave him a kiss on the cheek, and once Mia had taken off her boots, they raced upstairs. Joel arrived seconds after that, with a notepad tucked under his arm. He asked Kelsey to get her laptop, which meant they had to move to the kitchen.

Zach's stomach tensed, thinking about the clutter. But when he entered, his eyes snapped to Kelsey's.

"I'm getting there," she said, for his ears only. "But it's a lot."

"Get help," he whispered. She responded with a shrug, which suggested Kelsey was still going to try to do everything herself. Before joining Kelsey at the table, Zach spotted a child's drawing on the refrigerator.

It was a picture of two girls dressed in yellow sundresses, holding hands. One girl held on to a woman's hand and the other a man. Zach's heart warmed. Morgan saw him as part of her family. Then he got chills. Anyone who glanced at this picture would think that this was a family consisting of a mom, dad and children. A momentary panic rose within him. That should have been Sandy next to him. He shoved the panic to the recesses of his mind to focus on the custody case.

"So, this is what I was able to find out," Joel said, seating himself at the table along with Kelsey. Zach slipped into one of the two remaining chairs. "Frances Day, or Frankie, as she prefers to be called, got pregnant at sixteen years old. Her parents forced her to sign her daughters away. Now Frankie is a YouTube sensation, and she has thousands of followers. Frankie got famous reviewing products and trying them out. She's making good money and has secured a great attorney. Get this—Frankie's vlogging about her journey to reunite the girls. Thousands of people are rooting for her under the hashtag ReuniteMiaAndMorgan."

"Oh, my. This is worse than I imagined. Zach and I will be the monsters keeping the girls apart." Kelsey stood and swung her hands as her tears fell unheeded.

Zach retrieved the box of tissues from the coffee table and offered it to her while fighting his natural inclination. He wanted to hug her, to tell her everything would be okay.

Instead he said, "We can fight this," in a gentle tone, before returning to his seat to watch her pace.

"Who are you going to get to represent you?" Joel asked.

"Trent's seeing us tomorrow," Kelsey said, wiping her cheeks and rubbing her nose. "He's good, but I feel like we won't win against this mother. Judges love mothers. I could lose Morgan." She hiccupped as fresh tears began to fall.

In a swift move, Zach shot to his feet and went to pull her into his arms. She curved her body into his, sobbing into his chest. He inhaled the light scent of strawberries and gave her a pat on the back. Her tears whipped at his own concern, causing tremors in his stomach. A world without Mia would be equivalent to a world without the sun. For Zach, that was not an option.

"I can't lose her," she whispered, caught up in her grief. Then she shrugged out of his grasp. "How did she even find them?"

Joel, who had remained silent until now, cleared his throat. He wore a sheepish expression on his face. "It's the video. It went viral. Well, Frankie saw it, and…"

"I told you it was too soon to do that interview," she hurled. She looked ready to pummel the man. Zach reached out and snatched her arm in his.

"I had no way of knowing this would happen," Joel said, standing and holding up his hands.

"But it did," she shot back, her tone harsh. She cut her eyes at him.

Zach signaled to Joel to leave. The other man gathered his papers. "I didn't mean any harm," he said to Kelsey. "I just meant to celebrate them. That was all. And news like that wouldn't stay hidden for long in this day and age."

"I know…but I could lose her," Kelsey said in a more reasonable tone. She dragged her fingers through her curls. Joel gave her a pat on the back before letting himself out.

The urge to admonish her to pray built within Zach with huge force. Though he refused to obey, the words tore from him. "We won't lose our children if that's not in God's plan."

She gave a nod before asking a question that shook his inner core. "You're right, but if this is what God wants, what then?"

Chapter Sixteen

Trent West's office was as elegant as one would expect from the top attorney in the town. When Kelsey and Zach opened the door, the atmosphere in the lobby made her feel assured. Everything from the carpeting to the furniture was unparalleled in quality. Trent was doing well for himself, and it showed.

She noted the pleased glint in Zach's eye.

"Not bad for a small town, eh?" she whispered.

He nodded. "I've got to say I'm impressed."

Trent's personal administrative assistant, MaryAnn, greeted them and offered them water and coffee before they were escorted to his office. Once they completed the paperwork securing his services and had each paid their portion of his fees, Trent explained the particulars of the case, repeating most of what Joel had already told them. Kelsey, who had also received notification of the custody battle, had already scanned and emailed the case information to Trent's office.

"We will most likely settle this in mediation," he said, using a manicured index finger to adjust his glasses on the bridge of his nose, his perfect whitened teeth set in a wide grin. "I took the liberty of talking to one of my friends at the courthouse, and we've set a date for July 29, if that works for you?"

"Yes, that's wonderful," Kelsey said, pulling out her cell and plugging in that date. From the corner of her eyes, she could see Zach doing the same. Even though Trent's office was spacious, he had scooted his chair close to hers so that when they moved, their arms touched.

"That works for me," Zach said.

"Great. That's settled." Trent brushed at a speck of dust on his pants. "Be here a few minutes before 9:30 a.m. Have you viewed her YouTube channel?" he asked.

Both Zach and Kelsey shook their heads.

"She's evoking a lot of sympathy. Lots of people are rooting for her, and she has procured formidable representation." Trent straightened his tie and cocked his head. "Would you be agreeable to a shared custody agreement?"

Kelsey stiffened. "What do you mean?"

Zach straightened in his chair. "The only person I'm willing to share custody with is Kelsey." Her heart felt like melted chocolate at those words. She bit back a smile and struggled to remain focused on Zach's next words. "I get that this young woman's parents made the decision for her when she was a minor, but I don't know her. I don't know her lifestyle or if she's being genuine about wanting to be in their lives. She's an internet sensation. For all I know, this Frankie Day could be using the girls to get more followers. It could be a storyline. I'm very particular about whom I have around my child."

Now she had the fuzzies. Zach trusted her. His words implied it. His actions proved it. It was one thing to know it, but hearing it vocalized cemented it in her mind. Kelsey had to bite her inner cheek to keep her lips from spreading wide. She was usually more verbal, but her mind was like cotton balls at his words.

"Until I know her intentions—" Zach took Kelsey's hand in his "—and I think I can speak for both of us, we won't agree to shared custody." Her hand loved its new location, feeling warm and secure.

"Fair enough," Trent said, tapping a finger on his oversize desk and looking back and forth between them. "I would suggest you watch her channel over the next couple weeks and learn what you can about her. But think about that option. It might help things to go well."

"Our girls are only five years old, and they've already been through a lot. Both have lost the only mother they had ever known. Their little hearts have to be the priority," Zach said.

Wow. Kelsey sat deep in her chair, feeling goose bumps break out on her arms. Yet another thing the girls had in common. That realization gave her chills.

"I don't want them facing unnecessary trauma," he continued. "They need consistency and love. Both of which they have in abundance with Kelsey and me working together."

She dabbed at her eyes with her free hand, since Zach still held her other hand in a loose grip. She forced herself to speak with coherence, though Zach's sincerity had reduced her to mush. "Zach and I have done our best to ensure Mia and Morgan cultivate their relationship and strengthen their bond."

"You raise valid points," Trent said. "All of which I will take back to her attorney."

Kelsey cleared her throat. "I googled the law firm she's using. They seem...intimidating."

Trent waved a hand, appearing unconcerned. "Big fish. Little fish. All can still be eaten."

Despite the serious situation, Zach gave a small chuckle. "If you put it that way, I guess

I'll say make sure we're the ones doing the eating and not the other way around."

Trent nodded. "We are in agreement on that."

When they exited the building a few minutes later, Kelsey and Zach stopped in the parking lot. Shielding her eyes from the sun, she squinted up at him. "I feel good about Trent. Do you think we should let the girls know what's going on?" She chewed her lip. They were too young for all this upheaval.

"Yes, we should," Zach said, though he appeared hesitant. "I don't want to worry them, but if their biological mother ends up getting custody—though I can't imagine that happening—then we should prepare them as best as possible."

"You're a good dad," she said.

"So are you. A good mom, I mean."

Her stomach clenched. "Morgan called me Mom again. She goes back and forth between Auntie and Mom. Kind of like she's testing the waters to see how I respond. I haven't said anything, but it bothers me."

"Why?" he asked in a tender tone. Just then, a red sports car came into the parking lot passing them at high speed. Zach grabbed her arm and swung Kelsey out of the way.

She held her chest. "Oh, my. Thank you so much. She could have hit me." She had tingles up her arm from Zach's hand. The car swerved up to the front of Trent's building, and a tall, svelte blonde hopped out. Kelsey rolled her eyes. "She's acting like she owns the place."

"I think she does. I saw her picture in Trent's office," Zach said. "Are you all right?"

Hearing the concern in his voice made warmth snake up her spine. Warning herself not to show how pleased she was, Kelsey replied with a nod of the head. "To answer the prior question, I feel like I'd be taking Kennedy's place. I have no right to do that."

He touched her arm. He was being touchy-feely today, she noted, and she was enjoying it.

"You're not taking anybody's place. You're giving Morgan what she needs. Maybe she needs a mom."

He removed his hand from her arm, studying her with grave intensity.

"What about Mia?" she asked. "Does she need a mom?" Kelsey placed a hand over her mouth and stepped back. That sounded like an audition. Before Zach could utter a word, she said, "Forget I said that. I didn't mean it the way it sounded."

"I'm glad you didn't say that in the girls' presence," Zach said, rubbing his jaw. He didn't appear to be thrown by her comment. "You know they are trying to be matchmakers and put us together, right?"

"What?" she asked, putting her hand between them. Then her eyes went wide. She slapped her forehead. "That explains Morgan's picture on the refrigerator." Kelsey knew her cheeks were flushed.

"Yeah, I saw it the other day when I was over there. It caught me off guard." He cracked up, and Kelsey chuckled with him. "But don't blame Morgan. This is all Mia. She thinks she's so smart. She's the mastermind. I know it. Mia asked me if you're going to be her mother, and I told her no. But she's determined and persistent. I mean, can you imagine us being together?" He shook his head and gave her a light jab. "The other day I overheard them plotting for us to get together. Mia was trying to talk Morgan into telling you to marry me. As if that would ever happen? It was hilarious. I wished I had captured them on video for you to get a good laugh." His body shook with amusement until he had to wipe his eyes.

Kelsey kept a smile on her face. On the inside, an odd hurt began to form around her heart. He was acting like being with her would be ridiculous. A laughing matter. And hearing him gloss over telling Mia he wouldn't be with her pierced her tender feelings.

You're friends, she told herself. Just shake your shoulders and laugh it off.

But she couldn't.

So she did what she could.

Retreat.

Twisting away from him, she tossed over her shoulder, "Don't forget you're hosting movie night," and scuttled to her car.

From where he sat on the couch, Zach tried to capture Kelsey's attention, but she appeared to be engrossed in the movie on his seventy-inch screen. He had converted the basement into the ultimate family cave for himself and Mia. They all sat on the curved Milo Baughman sectional that was constructed of four pieces and could seat up to ten people. Zach was at one end, Kelsey on the other and the girls between.

Mia and Morgan were snuggled close together under a leopard-print blanket. Each had a hand dunked in the large bowl of popcorn. Like Kelsey, their eyes were glued to the screen. They were watching *It Takes Two*, and from the way their heads bobbed, this wouldn't be their only time watching the movie.

The girls loved watching movies and TV shows about twins now. *Sister, Sister* stayed on repeat in his house.

He cleared his throat during the scene where

the twins tried to rekindle a romance between their parents, but Kelsey didn't glance his way.

Zach narrowed his eyes and rubbed his chin. Come to think of it, she had been quiet at gymnastics last night. Except for when she had been on the phone, talking to someone and appearing agitated. However, when he asked, she'd told him she was okay.

Maybe he should try the direct approach. "Kelsey, do you want more popcorn?" he asked.

She met his eyes. Finally.

While she smiled and said, "I'm good, thank you," Zach studied her keenly.

He wanted—no, needed—to be close to her. He didn't know if it was because she was his one true friend so far in the small town, or if it was because she was the only person who could understand his feelings about finding his daughter's twin sister. Or, was it that they were about to face a situation where they could each lose their child? He didn't know for sure. He just knew he liked the connection.

He stood and gestured for her to join him out of the girls' earshot. Once she did, he whispered, "I know we planned to tell the girls after the movie, but after giving it some thought, I think the best thing for us to do is wait to see what happens at mediation. What if we tell them, get them all worked up and then the mediator decides to vote on our side?"

She was already nodding before he finished speaking. "Yes. Let's wait. I think that's a good idea," she said, sounding and looking like her normal self.

"So that's what we'll do," he whispered. "Are we in agreement?"

"Yes, I agree." Her smile was now generic, plastic, like a flight attendant greeting the queue boarding a plane. Her eyes became dull. Polite. Like he was anyone—or no one. Then she returned to the couch and refocused on the film.

He didn't like it.

He just didn't know what to do about it.

Morgan stood up, wiggling her body. "I've got to go." Judging by how she swung her hips like she was hula-hooping, he would say she had been holding it for a while.

Zach rushed to grab the remote and paused the movie.

"I'll go, too," Mia said, running after her sister.

Appreciative of a moment alone, Zach sat next to Kelsey and lifted her hand. "Is everything all right?" he asked.

"Why wouldn't it be?" Her voice was pleasant, but Zach had been married. He knew that tone. And he was prepared to apologize as soon as he knew what he had done wrong.

"Something's wrong," he said, holding a hand up when it looked like she was about to speak. "I can't put my finger on it, but I can feel it." He struggled to think of what he could have done to upset her. Replaying their last conversation, he remembered them laughing over the twins' attempt to bring them together.

Unless...

Maybe she hadn't found it funny. Maybe she'd gotten offended when she heard him praising Mia as being smart and not Morgan? He didn't know what to think.

"It's work," she said, raking a hand through her curls. Relief seeped through his body when he heard those words. "Gerald is up to his petty antics again. Stealing clients, playing dirty. I'm wondering if I shouldn't move once we've settled this custody dispute—which I am declaring we will win."

"Why should you have to find another spot because of him?" Zach said, hating to see her under any distress. "He's the one that relocated his office across from you. It's time to pray him out of your life."

She shook her head. "I wasn't talking about finding another spot here in town. I was talking about—"

Mia rushed in to tell Kelsey that Morgan needed her, thus ending the conversation and leaving Zach with a question. A question that made his heart pound, his palms sweat and his stomach fill with unease. Was Kelsey thinking of moving away to another state? And, if so, where did that leave Mia...and him?

Chapter Seventeen

She was tired of the pretense.

For two weeks, Kelsey had tried to smile and laugh and act normal around Zach after he had laughed about the thought of them being together. But the pretense was like a boulder on her shoulders, weighing her down. What was worse, she didn't understand why the hurt had grown like an ant's nest.

Trudging into Dr. Hernandez's office, Kelsey greeted the other woman before slipping into the sofa and dropping her purse on the floor beside her. This was her second session alone with the doctor, and she was determined to talk this time. During her first visit, the Friday after their movie night, she'd spent most of the time crying. And crying. Once she had stepped past the doorjamb, the walls that held her emotions at bay had crumbled, and she had broken down.

Thinking about her meltdown made Kelsey wrap her arms around herself in self-defense.

"How are you doing?" Dr. Hernandez asked, settling on the couch next to her. They sat in the doctor's office space reserved for adults. There was a huge round clock hanging across from her, a large window and a beautiful abstract that took up a large portion of the wall.

Focusing on the clock, her ears attuned to the tick of the second hand, Kelsey cleared her throat. "I'm doing… I just hope I can make it through another session without falling apart like I did the last time."

"You don't have to feel embarrassed. This is a safe place. Now let's make the most of our time together." Hearing the rustling of papers, Kelsey looked over at the other woman, who held a legal-size notepad on her lap and a pen in her left hand. After scanning her notes, she asked, "How's Morgan?"

"Morgan's doing fine, actually," Kelsey said, her mouth loosening. "I've been watching how I act around her, and it's really making a difference. By the way, thanks for fitting me in today. I appreciate it."

"Not a problem. I had a cancellation, so I was more than happy to fit you in. It's great hearing that Morgan's on a good path. I look forward to seeing her tomorrow night. How are you coping with caring for a five-year-old?"

"I moved into my sister's house, and the place is almost always a mess. Keeping the house clean is a major task. I can't keep up with that plus keep my business afloat."

"Believe me, I know. I have teenagers. Being a mother is a constant juggle." The doctor cocked her head. "Have you thought about hiring a housekeeper?"

Kelsey nodded. "Yes, but my sister never used one and she was able to maintain a spotless home while taking care of Morgan and her husband. I'm trying to do for Morgan exactly as Kennedy did." She burrowed deeper into the couch. "But, of course, I'm failing."

"You're not your sister and unlike Kennedy, you have a full-time job," the doctor pointed out in a gentle tone. "I heard you mention that you moved into your sister's home. Why did you do that? Why not move Morgan in with you?"

"I gave up my apartment because it seemed like the right thing to do. I thought it would be easier for Morgan to cope. I didn't want to uproot her from the life she had always known." Kelsey felt as if her responses were as abstract as the piece of art in front of her.

"I get that you have the best of intentions for

your niece, but you've got to be you. You can't lose your identity when you become a parent."

"Ugh, I know that, but I just want to do a good job. I'm trying to make this transition as effortless as possible for Morgan while honoring my sister's memory." She curled her hands into fists. "But I can't get this right. I feel like I'm failing her," she said, picturing the five loads of laundry waiting for her when she got home.

The doctor stood to get them both a small bottle of water. "You mention Morgan and your sister like this is only about them. Kelsey, this is also very much about you. You also experienced a loss. You're also going through a transition. Yet you are downplaying your feelings and your emotions. Why do you think you're doing that?"

"Because the last time it was about me, I took a life." Kelsey gasped and clasped her hands tight. Her revelation had shaken her to her core.

Dr. Hernandez arched her brow. "What do you mean?"

She looked down at her hands, twisting them together. "I'm talking about my mother. She died during childbirth. Having me. It's all my fault. It was her life or mine, and she gave hers." Her chin quivered. "If it weren't for me, my mother would be alive." Looking upward, she said, "That's why I don't understand why God took my sister and not me. She was the perfect mother. Perfect in everything. And me? I can't even remember to pack Morgan's lunch most days." Kelsey's shoulders shook as the tears fell.

"Let it out," the doctor soothed, rubbing her back and handing her some tissues.

Kelsey wiped her face and clutched the tissues in her hand. "I promised myself I wouldn't cry. Yet, here I am bawling my eyes out, and we're not even ten minutes in."

"That's quite all right. That's what this time is for. It's about you. Kelsey. No one else."

"Don't you see?" Kelsey wailed. "It shouldn't be about me. That's what I'm trying to say. Morgan is the one who lost her mother. Not me."

"But you did. And you're so busy blaming yourself that you refuse to allow yourself to grieve. You might have been a baby, but you did lose your mother."

"I had a wonderful stepmother," Kelsey said.

"It doesn't matter," the doctor said, shaking her head. "That grief has kept you from wanting to become a mother. Though you are worthy."

Kelsey touched her chest and exhaled. *Worthy.* No. She wasn't worthy.

"The key to love is that even when we feel we don't deserve it, God gives it to us in so many ways. You had a stepmother, and now

Morgan has you. That didn't just happen. That was God's intention."

She allowed the tears to fall and met the doctor's gaze. "Morgan's been calling me Mommy, and it scares me. Every time she calls me that, I want to hurl and rage. I'm not trying to take Kennedy's place. I don't want Morgan to forget her. It hasn't even been a year."

"You don't have to take Kennedy's place. The heart makes room. That's all Morgan is doing. Making room for you. She knows who Kennedy is, and yes, she did ask me if she could call you Mommy."

Kelsey's heart pounded. "She did? And you told her she could?"

"I told her it was okay for her to love you," Dr. Hernandez said. "It was okay for her to show you how much she cares about you."

Kelsey took a sip of water while she processed the doctor's words. Her heart squeezed, and her eyes widened. "Are you saying that Morgan's calling me Mommy because that's her way of expressing how she feels about me?" When the doctor nodded, Kelsey had to swallow the fresh tears. "I didn't see it that way."

"Sometimes we are so used to looking at things from our perspective, that we forget there are multiple points of view. Two people can be in the same situation, experience the same event, and see it in different ways. You need a paradigm shift." She adjusted her glasses before continuing. "For example, you see yourself as failing, while I see you as fighting. You could have chosen to run and have Morgan become a ward of the state. Instead, you made sacrifices to care for someone else, putting their needs above your own. That's a real parent. A mom. That's what I see."

Kelsey's heart warmed. She touched her chest. "You see all that in me after two sessions?" The question tore from her soul.

With a quick nod, the doctor answered without hesitation. "Yes. I do. And so does Morgan. Don't worry about where you think you're falling short. Love makes up the difference. So get yourself a housekeeper if you need one. That's small stuff," she said with a wave. "You said earlier your mom gave her life, but the truth is, she chose you. There was a choice between her life or yours, and she decided to put your life above hers. She chose you. And that was okay."

Overwhelmed, Kelsey could only nod as fresh tears became a cleansing. The guilt from her past began to leak out of her heart like pus from a sore. "I never looked at it that way," she finally managed to say.

The doctor smiled. "Sometimes to truly see the truth, all you have to do is change your focus."

"I don't think I could ever thank you enough for holding things down at the church and with the boys," August said, easing his body carefully into his chair. He was dressed in black lounge pants and a T-shirt, along with a pair of slides.

"I was happy to help," Zach said, admiring the beautiful hues of the approaching sunset and the large weeping willow swaying in the light.

Zach and August sat in armchairs in the sunroom of the pastor's home, located at the rear of the church. It was one of the landmarks of Swallow's Creek, and though over a hundred years old, it had been well maintained and modernized. There was a rumor that it had been a stop on Harriet Tubman's Underground Railroad, and if it were true, Zach wouldn't be surprised. While he visited with the pastor, Izzy had agreed to watch Mia and Morgan, since Kelsey had said she had an appointment.

"Every single person who has called or stopped by to see me has mentioned how much they enjoyed your messages. That's no surprise, considering this is your calling."

"Thanks for your kind words, but I'm relieved to return the reins to you," Zach said.

August rubbed his chin. "You could agree to be my copastor? I'm looking to get more ministries up and running. I want to get Bibles and food out to developing nations, and I need to start a program to help single mothers. But as the saying goes, the harvest is ripe but the laborers are few. What say you?"

Zach held up a hand. "This is it for me. I stepped in because you had surgery. Now that you're recovered, I'm done. I don't mind helping with the boys in juvie. We've been playing ball on Thursday mornings, which leads to minilectures and counseling, and I am happy to keep going with that because I've formed a bond with them. But I can't say yes to anything else."

"Can't? Or won't?" the other man challenged.

Zach scratched his head. "Both. I got to a place in my life where I couldn't continue to preach about things I no longer believe. I won't be a hypocrite—one who preaches one thing and lives another."

"If you don't mind my asking, how did you get to that place?" August asked. His tone held curiosity and concern. Not judgment. Which was why Zach didn't mind providing a response.

"When Sandy got sick, I prayed more than I ever had in my life. I fasted for days, hoping for God to save her. I know that everything is in His will, and I can respect that, but I exercised my mustard seed faith. That mountain should have moved. And when it didn't... I began to ask myself why was I leading people if my faith achieved nothing. If God didn't answer the prayer of my heart, then what about those who follow me?" Zach got choked up but refused to shed a tear. "I had to try to explain to a three-year-old that her mother wasn't coming back. That she was gone forever."

One defiant drop rolled down Zach's right cheek.

August had his fingers tented in his lap. "That must have been difficult," he said, then got quiet, like he was waiting for Zach to continue.

Zach was grateful for the silence, once again looking at the willow tree. The tree was bent low, swaying like an old woman carrying a load on her back. He could hear the whistle of the wind and scooted deeper into his chair.

He released a breath. "After Sandy...died, I tried to be like David. I tried to praise God anyhow. And I tried to be like Job and say, even if He slays me, that I would trust Him." His voice cracked. "I tell everyone I lost my faith, but the truth is, I couldn't trust myself. I had failed her. My prayers hadn't been enough. Sandy's last breath was spent begging me not to let her die...

and… I couldn't…" He covered his face with his hands as his control broke and tears trekked down his cheeks slowly, like soldiers returning from war in defeat.

A large hand rested on his back while he cried.

Even as the release came, Zach couldn't stop the words from pouring out. "Two young men in my church passed after that, and I… My prayers hadn't helped them, either." His shoulders hunched over with guilt.

And the tears continued.

There was no stopping the release.

"Go ahead," August whispered. "Let it heal. Let it deliver."

Zach staggered to his feet to make his way to the door. "I've got to go. I can't…"

August slipped around him to block his path. "You're not going anywhere. Today is the day God wants to absolve you of your guilt. You've been holding this like a camel holds water, and it's time for it to end."

"No," he said, grabbing August's shoulder. "I can't bear it."

"You're right," August said with steel in his voice. "That's what you get for doing God's job. For taking on God's burden. He said to cast everything on Him. Not take it on for yourself. Your job is to lead souls to Him. That's it."

"Why are you making me face this? I don't want to deal with this right now, if ever," Zach yelled. "I'm angry, don't you get that? I'm so mad I can't think straight."

"Finally!" August said, pumping his fists. "I've been waiting for this." He squared his shoulders and held Zach's chin. "Let it out. Let it out, my brother."

Bunching his fists, Zach felt a roar form low in his belly. The rage he had held would not be confined. It built and built as the pastor urged him on. Until Zach found himself shouting. Screaming. Raging at God.

Lifting his hands, Zach howled until he was hoarse and weakened before sinking to his knees. His heart felt ravaged, empty.

Ready.

It was then that August prayed for him, for forgiveness, for healing, for renewal.

This time new tears fell.

Washing over him like ointment on a cut.

His body shook with silent tears as his Friend began to speak to his soul, filling his heart with joy. With hope. With peace. When August was done praying, he pulled Zach to his feet.

"Thank you," Zach said, wiping his cheeks and chin before pulling August close to hug him tight.

August patted him on the back. "What are

you thanking me for? I didn't do anything. God did the work. And so did you. I didn't even break a sweat."

"I'm drenched," Zach said, pulling away.

"Yes. You need another washing, my brother," August said with a laugh. "And I don't mean the spiritual kind."

Chapter Eighteen

Since Kelsey had arrived at the mediation before Zach, she decided to busy herself with her crossword puzzle. MaryAnn had offered her coffee or tea, but Kelsey had declined. Digging in her bag, she was glad to find a pen with a cap she hadn't chewed. Some of the clues she had seen before, so after ten minutes she had filled in most of the squares. She crossed her legs and tapped her chin with the top of her pen.

Zach entered, bringing a nice waft of breeze with him. She got a whiff of sandalwood and orange, which her nose appreciated. He wore a white dress shirt and slacks, which coordinated with her black-and-white-striped dress. A nice coincidence. Kelsey greeted him before going back to her puzzle.

"I can't believe you beat me here," he said with a chuckle.

She tugged on her dress. "This was a good morning with Morgan, for which I was grateful."

"It will be all right," Zach whispered.

She arched a brow.

"You're doing your crossword and chewing your pen. I notice you do that when you're agitated or thinking."

Ugh. She snatched the pen cap out of her mouth. She hadn't realized she had chewed down another one. "I did a lot of praying last night and this morning," she said. "I was up at dawn. Couldn't sleep. I tossed and turned most of the night. But I'm determined to trust God and let Him work this out."

"It's okay to be nervous," he said, tapping her on the nose.

"I'm good." Kelsey shifted and turned away from him slightly. Not too much, so as to draw suspicion, but enough to allow her not to breathe in the scent of his cologne or see that lopsided grin on his face. She drew short breaths, unsure why her heart was racing. It couldn't be because he, too, had adjusted and now his hand rested next to hers. With a sigh, she tossed her crossword in her bag. Over the past couple weeks, she had been becoming more aware of him even though she spoke to him less. Being the friendly sidekick grated her nerves. But to admit it would mean questioning why…and she was not ready to figure out the puzzle of her mind.

So she directed her attention to the clock, which told her it was 9:27 a.m. Three minutes before their appointment time.

"I brought you this," Zach said.

She saw a piece of paper in her peripheral vision and turned to get a better look. She drew in a breath. He had cut out the Sunday paper's crossword puzzle. If her heart could make a sound, it would have said, *Awww*. Instead, she thanked him, keeping her tone neutral, warning herself not to get all emotional over a crossword puzzle…and ignoring the persistent, yet endearing thought that Zach had to have been thinking of her when he cut it out of the morning paper.

"Were Joel or any other press outside?" she asked.

"No. Trent told me they told the press an afternoon time to give us privacy."

"That was a good idea."

He coughed the kind of fake cough meant to get her attention. "Kelsey, this might come at you from way across the three-point line, but I have to ask. Are you avoiding me?"

She met his narrowed gaze. "Why would you ask that? We see each other every day, and our girls are always together."

"I don't know. It feels…a little cool between

us, and I'm not talking about the AC vent above our heads."

Of course she had to be cool. Otherwise, he might feel the one-sided heat that being around him generated in her, and she couldn't have that.

He cocked his head, those multicolored eyes staring at her with intensity. "Am I wrong?"

She straightened to keep from squirming and, on impulse, decided to tell him the truth, to express her feelings and give Zach a chance to say he didn't mean his words the other day. She was all too sure that would be his answer, especially after his thoughtful gesture of bringing her the crossword. Besides, she missed having meaty conversations with him. Kelsey licked her lips. "The reason—"

Just then, Trent sauntered in, ending their conversation. "Good morning," he said, holding a large coffee cup, the steam visible. Zach jumped to his feet, releasing her hand to shake hands with the attorney. For a moment, Kelsey didn't know what to do with her hand after it had lost its cozy spot, and it hung limply by her side. She trailed behind the men while they rambled on about the weather.

Then Zach stopped and held out an arm. Kelsey felt her eyes go wide when she registered his intention. But she looped her arm in his, appreciating how Zach held out the chair for her once they entered the conference room.

Her insides began to flutter as nervousness built, and she found herself reaching for Zach's hand. He gave her a light squeeze and a reassuring smile. Trent sat across from them and placed his coffee on a coaster.

"Before Ms. Day arrives, I wanted to give you both a few minutes so I can answer any further questions or concerns you might have," Trent said. They'd had a couple conference calls with him prior to today's meeting, and he had kept them updated via email.

Zach shook his head. "I don't have any questions, but my biggest concern is obvious. I don't want to lose my child." He clutched Kelsey's hand and looked her way, his gaze warm. "Let me rephrase. I don't want to lose any of my girls."

She knew she blushed. *My girls*. His comment felt like it included her, and there was no holding back her corresponding small smile.

"My stomach is in knots," Kelsey admitted, her voice quivering. "We haven't told the girls about this yet. But, this morning, as I was getting Morgan dressed, my heart squeezed. I thought to myself, this could be the beginning of the last time I get her clothes together, comb her hair, pack her lunch." She broke off and shuddered. "It's scary to think about. All the small moments became major. Treasured."

Zach pulled her into a brief hug, patting her on the back. "God has us. We have to trust Him."

Later, after the meeting, Kelsey would let herself think about the significance behind Zach's words—his sudden shift—but for now, all she could do was nod and sniffle in his arms until he released her.

Trent stood to get a tissue. "I know this isn't easy, but it will be okay. The mediator for today's proceedings, Raphael Cruz, is a retired family court judge who is trained in mediation. He's one I've worked with before, and I can tell you from experience, he's going to do what's best for the girls," he said, his tone sympathetic. "I hope that helps."

She gave a jerky nod and wiped her face. "I just hope I can keep it together." Then she did the opposite of her words and broke down. Her teeth chattered, and nervous tears trekked down her face.

MaryAnn poked her head inside. "The other party has arrived."

At her words, Kelsey bit her lower lip, trying to hold her disquiet at bay.

"I'll give you a few minutes to compose yourself," Trent said, standing and glancing at his watch. "Try to get yourself together while I go greet the other attorney and Ms. Day." He exited the room.

"I'm trying," she huffed out in jerky breaths as she faced Zach. "But Morgan's all I have. I..." She swallowed a sob, clamping her lips tight.

"You have me. We're in this together." Zach drew her close, and she rested her head on his arms, drawing from his silent strength. He plucked a few more tissues and wiped her eyes and cheeks.

Kelsey thanked him and stood. "Let me go wash my face and blow my nose." She lowered her eyes, hating her scattered emotions. She had hoped to remain poised throughout the meeting, but her heart was in panic mode.

She entered the bathroom, which had a soothing vanilla scent, and blew her nose. Standing in front of the mirror, she cupped her splotchy cheeks. She could see the fear behind her reddened eyes. Closing her eyes, she uttered a quick prayer to God for strength. Then she washed her face with cold water, squared her shoulders and reentered the conference room.

He liked her.
Yes, he did.
Zach liked the woman who wanted to take his child from him.

When Frankie Day entered the room dressed in a white blouse, plaid skirt, thigh-high socks and Mary Jane shoes, Zach had gasped. He knew from the YouTube videos that Frankie looked like an older version of the girls, except her hair had been dyed gray with streaks of pink. But seeing her in person made the resemblance striking. Hearing her speak made her endearing. He understood why Frankie had won over the hearts of so many followers.

Right now, her eyes shone as though they brimmed with unshed tears. She had asked to address them after both attorneys had presented their opening statements. "When that video came across my screen, I couldn't believe it." She put a hand to her chest. "I had dreamed of finding my daughters one day, but my parents had opted to do a sealed adoption. By the time I got old enough, the original agency had closed." The tears fell. "Thankfully, you posted that video. I wouldn't have found my little girls otherwise. My babies."

He felt chills. Actual chills. Like the ones you get at the end of a feel-good film. However, in this case, he didn't want to cheer. This was his life and his child's.

As if on cue, the outside darkened, and a crack of thunder boomed.

He heard Kelsey's indrawn breath and glanced

her way. Once she had returned from the bathroom, she had remained quiet, her only words to say a quick hello to the other occupants in the room. He saw her lips twist and reached a hand under the table to join his with hers again, which felt...right.

Frankie pierced her gaze their way. "Thank you so much for taking care of my daughters. They were blessed to have you in their lives. I'm so glad they ended up with good..." She appeared to search for a word, any word that wouldn't acknowledge the fact that Mia and Morgan had parents. "Caregivers," Frankie finally said.

Kelsey leaned forward and stabbed an index finger on the top of the table. "We're more than caregivers. This wasn't a foster home situation. Zach is Mia's father. And I... I am—" She faltered and licked her lips before squaring her shoulders. "—her m-m—I'm Morgan's family."

Her words appeared to douse Frankie's enthusiasm. The other woman shook her head. "I—I know that. I didn't mean to imply that..." She trailed off and swallowed. Her eyes were wide. Innocent. Trusting. Zach had to look away.

"We know what you meant," Zach said, squeezing Kelsey's hand.

Kelsey swallowed. "Zach's right. Thank you for your kind words. Yes, the girls are both loved, and we have done our best to keep them together."

Frankie slouched her long frame, hugging herself. "I'm sorry for upsetting your lives— their lives. But I'm in a good place. I never wanted to give them up, and I think my parents had the girls placed with separate families to keep me from finding them. This is my chance to have them both under one roof." Her chin quivered. "Which is why I'm here. My girls deserve to be together. With me." She straightened, touched her abdomen and whispered, "That's how they've been from the start."

She had them there. In uniting them, Frankie would make both girls happy beyond measure. He clamped his jaw and silently prayed to squelch the rising apprehension gnawing within him. He could lose his child, he realized, his legs weak. The baby he had held in his hands from three days old. The toddler he had watched take her first step. The girl he had hushed when she had lost her first tooth...and her mother.

Oh, Sandy.

Zach was glad she wasn't here to experience this dread. To see his failure. His inability to keep his promise and care for their child. Worry chomped at his gut, leaving him raw.

Kelsey's face mirrored his trepidation. He had heard the expression about tasting fear, but Zach had never understood it until that moment. It tasted like…castor oil. Unpleasant. Lingering. Staying on his tongue.

Zach's stomach churned, and his chest heaved. Kelsey leaned into his chest as if she had lost the ability to remain upright. He slung an arm around her shoulder and reminded himself to breathe. Inhale. Exhale. Inhale. Exhale. He felt like he was drowning under the abyss of fear. Memories of Mia's formative years flashed before him. Kisses. Hugs. Tears. Laughter. Hurt. Through all of those, he had been there. And to go from that to being…out of the picture.

No.

He couldn't let that happen.

But who would snatch children from a mother who lost them through no fault of her own?

Trent jumped in. "Ms. Day, your desire for your girls to be together is a reality. Pastor Johnson and Ms. Harris have made every effort to ensure that the girls bond. They spend time together every night. Like a family."

"Like a family is not the same as being with their real mother. She's their family," Greg Weidner, Frankie's attorney, said.

His words made Kelsey snap. "Real mother? Really?" She swung a head Frankie's way. "Excuse me for saying this, because you seem like a nice person, but being a parent is more than biology." Zach prodded her to stop, but Kelsey halted his efforts. "No, I've got to say what's in my heart," she huffed out. "Being a parent is knowing the little things that are actually not little but major. Like Morgan's favorite color. What she likes to eat. To sing." Her voice went tender. "How she insists I read her two stories before bed. That's what makes a mother."

"I didn't get to do that, and I wanted to real bad. I made some mistakes, but I loved my girls." Frankie plopped her head on the table, her shoulders heaving. Her sobs filled the room. Though Greg tried to comfort her, Frankie was inconsolable. It was like she had saved all the tears from the last five and a half years to release them at this moment.

And it poured.

A mother mourning for time she would never recover. Years forever gone like a speck of dust in the wind. Years that could never be reclaimed.

God seemed to cry with her, releasing a heavy downpour, its sound accompanying her tears with a dissonant chord. Zach rubbed his temples, a headache forming.

"This is not an easy situation," the mediator said, attempting to speak above Frankie's wails and the sounds of the thunderstorm. "I can understand both sides…" He trailed off.

Trent asked Raphael for a recess and returned with more bottles of water.

Kelsey cracked under Frankie's breakdown, rushing out of the room. Zach's heart twisted. A strong desire to lay hands on the young woman and pray for her grew until it thundered in his ears. He fought it, closing his eyes and thinking of Kelsey, who was in the bathroom crying.

From where he sat, Zach only had to turn his head in order to see Trent and Greg conferring with the mediator. After a nod, the judge popped inside to state any attempt to continue the mediation that day would be futile. He promised to deliberate and review their case before setting another date of August 8. After some effort, Greg was able to assist Frankie out of the room.

Zach lowered his head, his cheeks wet as the tears rolled down his face.

This was a case in which there could be no real winners. All he could do was whisper, "Fix it, Jesus." Because there was a 100 percent certainty that everyone in this battle would have scars. And Mia and Morgan were the ones who would suffer most.

Chapter Nineteen

She wished she could choose another day to do this, especially after the day she'd had. Kelsey stood by the window of her living room, watching out for Zach and Mia's arrival.

She'd had to reschedule two closings because of a broken pipe in one house and an electrical repair in the other. Suspicious, as both houses had passed inspections. Kelsey was convinced this was Gerald's underhandedness, but she couldn't prove it. She could, however, place this into God's hands. So she had reached out to Sienna and Jade to pray. Then she had spent the rest of the afternoon debating her next move.

She sighed, massaging her neck. No use putting off a much-needed conversation. After the mediation yesterday, Kelsey and Zach had decided to tell the girls, especially since the media had contacted both of them for a statement. Neither of them wanted the girls to hear about the lawsuit from someone else.

Kelsey moved to fluff the pillows on her couch, then turned to admire her shiny furniture and freshly vacuumed space. Coming into a clean house after a day like today was a blessing. Her new housekeeper came twice a week, and each time, Gwyneth left the house smelling like fresh linen. Kelsey returned to her spot by the window.

A minute passed before Zach's truck pulled into her driveway. Once he had parked, Zach opened the door and helped Mia out of the vehicle. He took her little hand in his, and Mia glanced up at him with a smile. That small action of trust made Kelsey's eyes well. She sniffled and wiped her tears.

After she unlocked her front door, Kelsey stood at the foot of the stairs and called out to Morgan.

"I'm coming, Auntie," she yelled.

Yes, yelled.

The moment was bittersweet.

Kelsey prayed this new development wouldn't lead to a setback in her niece's well-being. Zach and Mia came inside, each giving her a hug. She lingered longer than necessary in Zach's arms, placing a hand on his chest.

"We've got this," he whispered in her ear.

All she could do was nod.

"Morgan!" Mia exclaimed, hugging her sister close.

Morgan kissed her on the cheek. "I missed you so much, sissy!"

Kelsey chuckled and ruffled their hair.

Zach said, "If I didn't know better, I would think it was weeks they hadn't seen each other instead of a couple hours."

Forcing cheer into her tone, Kelsey said, "Girls, let's sit on the couch. We have something we need to talk to you about."

"Okay," Mia said, doing a shimmy. "This is going to be good."

"I can't wait," Morgan said, curling her hands into fists and shaking them.

Once they were seated, Kelsey sat beside them. Zach sat on the other side. Two expectant faces turned toward her with shiny eyes, their feet pumping against the couch. She stole a glance at Zach, her heart skipping a beat when she saw he was looking at her. With intensity.

She coughed, then raked her fingers through her curls, realizing there was no good way to begin a discussion like this one.

Praying for the right words, she said, "Girls, you both know you're adopted…" Two heads nodded. She paused, wishing she had practiced how to say this. Zach smiled and gave her a thumbs-up. "What that means is another lady gave birth to you." Two heads bobbed again. Great. It was going well so far. She squared her shoulders. "That lady saw a video of the both of you together, and guess what? She wants to meet you."

Their eyes went wide. "She wants to meet us?" they asked in unison.

"Yes. Do you think that might be fun?" Kelsey asked, faking her enthusiasm.

"Will you be there?" Morgan asked.

"Daddy, too?" Mia chimed in.

"Yes, I will be there, and so will Kelsey."

Morgan's next question made goose bumps pop up on her arms. "Are we going to have to live with her?"

Panic squeezed her vocal cords shut. Kelsey signaled to Zach to answer, drawing a deep breath. She gripped the edge of the couch.

"We don't know," Zach said with sadness. Kelsey could see how it pained him to utter those words, and she moved to sit next to him. Zach wiped his brow. "Your mother's name is Frankie, and she says she loves you very much. She wants to take care of you, so she went to a court to ask if she could get you back."

"You don't want us anymore?" Mia asked in a tiny voice.

Mia's question made Kelsey's heart squeeze.

Zach reached to grip Kelsey's hand, his shoulders hunched.

"We want you," Kelsey said. "We don't want you to leave us, but the mediator might say we have to let you go."

"I don't want to go, Mommy Auntie," Morgan said. Her body shivered, and her eyes held genuine fear.

Kelsey bit the inside of her cheek to keep from making promises she might not be able to keep. "I don't want you to go, either."

"What if we tell the memiator we don't want to go?" Mia asked.

"Mediator," Zach corrected.

"Yes," Morgan said, nodding.

"Frankie is your real mother," Zach said, sounding downhearted. Kelsey bristled at that word, *real*, biting her lower lip. "Though we love you very much, the court may decide that she's the best person to take care of you."

Morgan dissolved into tears. "No, she's not. You are." She crawled into Kelsey's lap.

"One good thing would be that you and Mia would live together," Kelsey said. "Would you like that?"

Morgan nodded. "But I want you."

Tears flowed down Kelsey's face.

Mia tapped her father on the shoulder. "If you and Ms. Kelsey got married, she could be my mommy. Then I could tell the memi—I mean mediator, I already have a new mommy, so I don't need another one."

"Oh, honey." Zach scooped Mia into his arms and hushed her.

"I want Kelsey to be my mommy, too," Morgan said, her face stained with tears. "Mr. Zach, will you be my daddy?"

"I wish I could be," he said, kissing Morgan on the cheek.

Kelsey rested her head on Zach's shoulder. Seeing the girls hurt and hearing their questions shook her very core.

"But you know what I can do? I can pray. I can pray for God to help us. Do you want to pray with me?" he asked the girls.

The girls gave a solemn nod. Kelsey's heart expanded, hearing Zach seeking God for direction. Because God was the only One they could turn to for assistance with this decision.

All four of them slipped to their knees. Then Zach prayed. His fervent prayer gave Kelsey hope. A hope she would try to hold on to no matter how bleak she felt.

She opened her eyes to observe Zach. He had his hands clasped, and he spoke to God with earnestness on all their behalf. She could hear his love. His passion. His trust. Zach began to worship God. Kelsey could hear his hunger, his thirst, and knew she wanted more of what he had.

And that's when her heart tripped.

In the parking lot.

Zach read Kelsey's text and slipped his phone in the pocket of his basketball shorts. He had been on his way to meet with the boys at the church when Trent called stating the mediator had reached a decision. Trent also told Zach that he needed to meet with both Zach and Kelsey first.

Slipping into one of the chairs in Trent's office, Zach commanded his heart rate to slow down. Trent went over to the large television screen and pulled up the YouTube app. He'd just begun typing in the search tab when Kelsey stormed in.

"What's going on?" she said.

Her curls flowed over her shoulders, and she was dressed in a formfitting dress with a beautiful shade of purple on her lips. Zach's breath caught. She looked extra beautiful. Like she had a lunch date? Zach hadn't heard her mention dating anyone. He frowned. He didn't like it.

She sat in the chair away from Zach. He didn't like that, either.

Trent froze the screen. "Raphael Cruz will

be here in about ten minutes. Frankie and her attorney are already in the conference room. I wanted to bring a delicate matter to your attention that I want to bring before the judge. There's a video…"

Kelsey groaned, "I hope this isn't Joel's interference again."

"What kind of video?" Zach asked.

"I'll let you see for yourself." Trent pressed Play.

Zach squinted. A young woman stood between two men, holding a cup in her hands, gyrating her body. She flailed her hands, spilling the liquid on herself and the men. Zach shook his head. She was drunk.

"That's Frankie," Kelsey gasped, leaning forward.

"Yes. She's a public figure. Someone recorded her and posted it to Instagram. This was a couple nights ago, and I believe it could sway things in our favor."

Kelsey nodded and swung around to face Zach. "What do you think?"

Zach placed a hand on his chin. He should be rejoicing.

"There's nothing to think about. If you want to win, we need to show the mediator this video. I can bet this isn't the first time she has behaved in that manner. It will discredit Frankie in a big way," Trent said. "She's not fit to be a mother."

"Who is?" Kelsey said, shaking her head.

Trent pursed his lips. "It's your decision, but for the record, I think this is God helping you out."

Zach didn't think so. "The problem is, that's my daughter's biological mother. What she needs is guidance. Not to be shamed."

"She did it to herself," Trent shot back. He stuffed his hands in his pockets, visibly trying to regain his composure. "Take a few minutes to talk it out and think about it."

Once he left the room, Kelsey gave a small smile. "I don't think Frankie is ready for motherhood." She sat next to him and rested her hand on his arm. "That video proves it."

"Watching her on the screen, all I see is a young woman in need of guidance, of help, of a relationship with God," Zach said.

"I understand your point. I think the solution is that we try to reach an agreement with her," Kelsey suggested. "Maybe give her an open invitation once she has gotten her act together."

He released a breath. "I don't think she would be amenable to that. She wants full custody."

Kelsey lowered her head. "I get that you're drawn to Frankie, and like everyone else, she deserves redemption and compassion, but she's grown and ultimately responsible for her actions. The girls can't speak for themselves. They are minors, and I need to be 100 percent certain they are going to be okay. We have to advocate for what is best for them."

She was right. Their daughters wouldn't be in a good situation right now in their mother's care.

"Okay. We'll show the video only if we have to. Let's see what the mediator says."

She gave a nod.

Trent ducked his head inside. "The mediator is here. What did you decide?"

Zach and Kelsey joined hands, and Zach told him their decision. Trent gave a terse nod and spun out of the room. They followed him into the conference room.

Frankie was already present with Greg Weidman. They sat across from her. Frankie was dressed in a black dress and glasses. He was having a hard time seeing her as the same young lady from that video.

The mediator began the proceedings. "I've given this matter serious thought, and I think it is in the best interest of the girls for them to get to know their biological mother. Ms. Day was cheated of the opportunity to be a mother, and I believe she deserves the chance. I will set the first meeting for a few weeks from now, and then we will begin transition to their new home."

Frankie clutched her chest, her face brightening with joy. Zach's gut wrenched. Sorrow began to weave around his heart.

Kelsey burrowed close and linked her arm through his, clinging to him. He could hear her quiet sniffles.

Trent adjusted his tie and cleared his throat. "Your Honor, I'm duty bound to act on my client's behalf. There is new information I would like to present..." He looked Zach's way and raised a brow.

To Zach's surprise, Frankie spoke up—interrupting Trent.

"I think I know what he's talking about," she said in a whisper. "There's a video of me, dancing, drunk in the club, going around. It isn't something I normally do, but I was...stressed. Nervous. And I did something dumb. I wanted to tell you, but I was advised it would ruin my chances. Please don't change your mind because of that. I love my girls." Her voice broke.

Raphael peered at Frankie above the rim of his glasses. Mr. Weidner pulled up the video for the mediator to watch. Raphael tapped his finger on the conference table as he perused the incident.

Zach tensed as he waited.

"Your Honor. The girls need to remain with us," Kelsey said once the video ended. "That's the best option. But we would love to give Ms. Day open visitation if she's agreeable."

The mediator addressed Ms. Day. "I applaud your efforts to be reunited with your daughters, but I'm going to recommend you take parenting classes. Then we will revisit this matter in three months. In the meantime, the girls will remain with their respective parents, and you can have biweekly visits for one hour. Supervised by the girls' parents."

Frankie nodded. "Thank you." Her tone was humble.

Zach and Kelsey exchanged contact information with Frankie and walked out of the building together.

"We still have them," he said to Kelsey, pulling on her soft curls.

"For now," she said, sounding dejected. "In three months, we'll have to face this all over again."

"Now, after the summer we have had, we both know a lot can happen in ninety days. That video came up overnight. We had no idea it would give us more time. So let's not limit what God can do." He cocked his head. "This might sound foolish, but I feel led to help Frankie."

Her eyes narrowed. "What do you mean?"

"I can feel it in my spirit that she's hurt, and I've been led to pray for her. I think she needs some good counsel."

Kelsey's eyes went wide. "She does. But does it have to be you?"

He nodded. "God brought her into my life—our lives—for a reason, and I don't believe the twins are the only reason. The two times I have been in Frankie's presence, I felt a strong urge to minister to her. She's in pain, and God wants to deliver her. Frankie believes that the twins will heal her heart, but only God can do that. Only He can wipe away her tears. For good." His chest heaved. "This is something I have to do, Kelsey. I know we're on opposite sides in this case, but Frankie's not the enemy. She's lost. Trapped in the pain of her past. And if God means for Mia and Morgan to be with her, we'll have no choice but to accept that. It won't be easy, but one small comfort would be knowing they were with someone who is whole, who has a relationship with God. I've got to help her. Please say you understand."

Zach wiped his brow, waiting. Hoping.

He needed a sign that she did indeed understand.

Kelsey moved into his space and ran a finger against his cheek. Then she grabbed his head between her hands and crushed her lips over his.

Caught off guard, Zach remained limp, unmoving.

She tore her lips away from his. "Say something," she huffed, chest heaving. "Say you feel what I'm feeling."

He opened his mouth, but no words came out.

Her eyes clouded over, and she twisted away from him, covered her face and ran. The only thing he registered was the click of her heels against the pavement. His heart screamed for him to call her back, let her know he'd made a mistake. But he wouldn't.

Zach had lost his wife, whom he'd loved.

He was about to lose his daughter.

He couldn't take the chance and lose out again.

Chapter Twenty

"Oh, my. Did you do it right?" Sienna asked. "You've been out of practice."

After she left Zach in the lot, Kelsey had sent out a 9-1-1 text to Sienna and Jade. All three women were now gathered in her kitchen. Sienna had prepared three huge bowls of sherbet, but Kelsey's remained untouched. Kelsey paced while she recounted the events leading up to her humiliation in between crying spurts.

Kelsey whirled around. "Of course I…" She trailed off, realizing Sienna wasn't serious. She was trying to ease the tension in the room.

"I'm surprised he just stood there like a wet noodle," Jade said. "You two seemed to have a connection."

Her voice broke. "We do, but it's centered around the girls." She slapped a hand to her forehead. "I can't believe I kissed him."

"Do you regret it?" Sienna asked.

"What kind of question is that?" Jade shot back. "Look at her. She's mortified."

Kelsey went over to stand by her friends. "I have no idea how I'm supposed to face him after today. I should have kept my lips to myself. But, at the same time, though it hurts—like stubbing your pinkie toe bad—I don't have any regrets."

Sienna stood to rub her hand across Kelsey's back. "What are you going to do?"

"I can't face him," Kelsey admitted, burying her face in her hands.

"Then don't," Jade chimed in, flanking Kelsey's other side.

Kelsey lifted her head. "There's no avoiding Zach. Did you forget about Mia and Morgan? I can't keep them apart."

Sienna shook her head. "This is a mess. Maybe take a week or two to clear your head. Jade and I can each take turns watching Morgan to distract her."

"Yeah, we could take her to the park, for ice cream..." Jade suggested.

Kelsey knew their tactic would fail, but she nodded, unable to think of another suggestion. There was no way Morgan would tolerate being apart from her sister for any amount of time.

Then Sienna gasped and stepped back.

"Kelsey, did you fall in love with Zach?" she asked. "Please tell me you didn't."

Her question slammed into Kelsey's chest, taking her breath. She shook her head. "No. No. I can't be. It was just a kiss." Wasn't it? She touched her lips as if they held the answer. Was she in love?

"You don't normally go around kissing people," Jade said, squinting her eyes, studying Kelsey before placing a hand on Kelsey's forehead. "It might be love."

"I don't think love comes with a temperature," Sienna said in a wry tone.

Both women huddled around her.

"Stop looking at me like I'm a new species from outer space," Kelsey said, giving a small chuckle despite her aching heart.

Sienna gave her a light shove. "You did fall in love. I can't believe you. What about the Three Divas and our motto, All for God, for Life? How could you?"

"She couldn't help it," Jade defended. She held a hand over her chest and said in a soft voice, "Did you ever feel this way with Christian?"

Kelsey shook her head, struggling to remember the last guy she had dated. "Not even close," she said in a hoarse voice.

"I think it's romantic." Jade sounded dreamy.

It would be romantic if her feelings had been reciprocated. But they weren't. Zach had shown exactly what he felt for her: nothing. Kelsey dropped into one of the chairs, struggling to breathe. If this was what real love felt like, she could do without it. "I've got to get out of here. I can't stay in this town. I can't be around him." San Diego. That's where she could go. Its sunshine would be the perfect remedy for the dimness of her heart.

"What?" Jade screeched. "You can't be serious."

"Love's not something you can run away from," Sienna said. "Which is why it should be avoided in the first place."

"You think I would do this to myself on purpose?" Kelsey shot back.

"Kelsey, you're not thinking straight. You just said a few minutes ago that you can't separate Morgan from her sister," Jade pointed out. "That wouldn't be right, and you could lose the girls if you did that."

"I'm putting the house up for sale. I can't stay close to him, seeing him every day." Yes. That's what she could do.

"That's a good idea. This house isn't you, anyway. You can move into my apartment building," Sienna said, brightening. "A two-bedroom opened up next to me."

"Listen, you need to slow down and not make any hasty decisions," Jade advised. "You fell in love, but you're not dying or on your last breath."

"It sure feels like it," Kelsey said, slumping her shoulders.

Sienna made a face before taking a step back. "I hope this isn't contagious."

Jade rolled her eyes. "Quit your nonsense. You're so dramatic."

"I feel like a fool for kissing him," Kelsey said. His rejection stung, pricking at her tender heart. "He's obviously still in love with his wife. I don't know why I thought…" She sniffled. "My heart feels like it's being ripped and torn to shreds." She broke into tears. "This is agony."

"I know. I've been there," Jade soothed. "But I got past it, and so will you. Believe me. You're stronger than you know, and you just have to press forward. Sienna and I will help you."

"I don't know if I will get past this," Kelsey said, shaking her head.

"You will. Eat your sherbet." Sienna nudged the bowl of iced treat toward her and wiped Kelsey's face. "We'll get past this together, one scoop at a time."

All he saw was a For Sale sign.

Those two words in bold had sucker punched him, and all Zach could do was smile and wave like he hadn't been shaken. Zach helped Mia out of his truck and kissed her goodbye. "I'll see you later, baby," he said. Mia nodded and skipped up the driveway.

Jade had given him a not-so-friendly wave before hugging Mia and closing the door to Kelsey's home.

Effectively shutting him out.

Since that day in the parking lot when Kelsey had kissed him, he had yet to see her face. Instead, Jade or Sienna had been the ones to juggle the girls between them, while he and Kelsey had communicated by text. He missed talking to her, hearing her voice. Kelsey was getting both girls ready for their one-hour visit with Frankie. Zach would meet up with Frankie later at MacGrady's without Kelsey. That didn't sit well with him.

They were a team. They were friends.

Or had been. Until that kiss.

Zach hadn't had the courage to confront her about his lack of response, because what could he say?

His heart pounded at the revelation that Kelsey might be moving.

He hoped it wasn't because of him.

He knew it was because of him.

Mia had talked about them making s'mores together, and as he drove away from Kelsey's home, Zach felt jealousy stir within him. His daughter was able to spend time in her presence, and he couldn't.

Or wouldn't.

He groaned. This was an added complication he hadn't expected. Complication? Guilt made him squirm. Kelsey was no complication. She was... Zach paused, though his heart pleaded with him to continue down that path. He had no right thinking about her or how right she felt with him, but his fear was stronger. Fear of opening his heart. He was never doing that again.

His heart might have been closed, but his mind was in overdrive.

Thoughts of her bold move consumed him.

Zach headed toward the church, trying to push Kelsey from his mind. Sandy had been the love of his life. Yet he couldn't remember what it felt like to kiss her. Their interactions were now a distant memory, replaced with a curly-haired, beautiful woman whom he ached to touch, to see her smile. And yes, to get another chance to return that kiss that had seared through the walls of his heart.

He slammed the steering wheel.

It was that For Sale sign. All he could visualize was that sign planted in the earth in front of Kelsey's house. Zach turned on his music to drown out his thoughts until he arrived at the church.

Exiting his vehicle, he stalked into the building toward August's office. Zach needed a listening ear. He found the pastor tinkering on the drums. When August saw Zach, he waved him in.

"What brings you here?" August asked. He looked at his watch. "Did we have a meeting I forgot about?"

"I was in the area and saw your truck. Thought I'd stop by."

August gave him a knowing look. "What's on your mind, friend?" He placed the sticks on the drum and sauntered to his desk.

Zach lowered himself into one of the chairs and groaned. "Everything. And Kelsey."

"Ah. I see." The other man nodded. "I should have known this was about a woman."

"Not just any woman." Zach lifted a brow. "I bet you know all about that?"

"Oh, no. Been there, tried that. Can't even write that story." Zach heard a slight note of pain, but August shrugged it off. "What happened with Kelsey?" he asked.

"She…she kissed me."

"Hmm…" The pastor rubbed his chin. "I take it that wasn't a good thing?"

"No. Yes." Zach lowered his head. "I have a wife."

"Had. You had a wife," August said.

"Sandy was my best friend. I loved everything about her. To move on so soon would diminish that."

"How?"

Zach didn't have an answer. "I don't know, man. I'm all confused."

"No. You're scared. Scared to put yourself out there."

"I can't lose another spouse," Zach said.

"She kissed you. She didn't propose," August jested, kicking back in his chair. "Maybe she wanted to see if you were her frog. Maybe that was it."

"No. That kiss was like a crackle of electricity. It was more."

"It awakened something you thought was dead?"

He nodded before he shook his head as realization dawned. "She didn't awaken anything. She's making me acknowledge it. And I wasn't ready to, but now she's leaving. I just saw that she put her house up for sale. How could she be so quick to skip town, like what we had was nothing?"

"Are you listening to yourself?" August asked. "You're all confused."

"If I sound that way, that's because I am." Zach jumped to his feet and paced the room. "Things were going good. We developed a solid friendship. Our daughters hang together every day. I don't see how she could be so willing to give all that up."

"It doesn't sound like she's trying to give anything up, my brother. It sounds like she is seeking more. As she should."

Zach stopped to look at August. "You're right, but I can't be that person."

"If you feel that way, then why are you here? Why is it bothering you that she is looking to relocate? You should be helping her pack."

"I don't want her to leave," Zach snapped. He clamped his jaw and stewed. Now he was second-guessing his decision to talk to August.

"Then what do you want?" August grew serious and leaned forward. "Do you love this woman? If you do, you'd better do something about it."

"It wouldn't be fair, because I can't love her like I did Sandy."

"Who said she wants you to? Love is the most powerful emotion in this world, and you're limiting it. You're acting like it cannot expand, reshape and reinvent itself into something better. Something…more. I've seen you together. You know the truth, and you need to be honest with yourself and admit it."

Zach departed shortly after that to pick up the girls, his mind chewing on the pastor's words. When he arrived at Kelsey's house and saw the sign on her lawn, a feeling of dejection clouded over him. Mia and Morgan bounded out of the house, wearing identical pink sundresses and tan sandals. Their hair was pinned in buns with large pink bows. Zach thought they looked beautiful. He backed out of her driveway and made his way to MacGrady's.

"I wish Ms. Kelsey was here," Mia said, her lips downturned.

"Me, too."

Me three. Zach swallowed.

Kelsey should be coming with them. She should be by his side. His heart ached, missing her on a deep level. One that couldn't be ignored. He remained silent, listening to the girls' chatter, until they were in front of the diner.

Gathering the girls, Zach headed inside. Once they got to the booth, Zach tried to fix Mia's hair, which had come undone.

"You're not doing it right, Daddy," Mia said. "You need Ms. Kelsey."

Zach froze. He did need her. This wasn't about want. It was about need. And he needed Kelsey. She was like a cool shower after a day spent on the basketball court. You know what else he needed to do? He needed to kiss that woman so she would know he was no frog. He was her prince. Or he wanted to be.

He counted every minute of the hour he waited for Frankie to show up for her scheduled visit. Yet, she never did.

Zach rushed back to Kelsey's house and rang the doorbell, the girls crowded around him. She opened the door.

"What are you doing here?" she asked, standing by the doorjamb and eyeing him with suspicion.

He zoned in on her glossy lips, snatched her close to him and kissed her, ignoring Mia's and Morgan's giggles. He pulled away much too soon, but he had to catch his breath.

Kelsey's eyes were warm and soft. "What was that about?"

Before he could answer, Mia said, "Daddy needed you to do my hair."

"Is that what I am to you?" Kelsey whispered, her voice trembling. "A convenience?"

"No, of course not." Zach shook his head. "I missed you. That's all."

"No. You missed what I do for you and Mia." She pulled away from him. "Until this very moment, I didn't realize that I was hoping. Hoping you would come to your senses, kiss me and tell me that you love me. But I can see that isn't going to happen."

Zach tried to talk, but she refused to listen.

Kelsey grabbed Morgan close and shooed him out the door. "I can't do this. I won't do this. Like, why should I be content to rent when I have the money to buy? I deserve better, and I won't settle for anything less than 100 percent."

He gathered Mia in his arms and stepped outside. "But what about the girls?"

"I'm done. Just stay away from me. Stay away from my child. Goodbye, Zach. I love you, Mia." Then she shut the door.

Chapter Twenty-One

Ugh. The birds had no right to be singing this morning. Not after the night she had endured. Morgan had cried herself to sleep right along with Kelsey. Kelsey lay on her back on her bed, wishing she could stay in this position forever. But she had a little person who needed her. She scuttled out of bed and trudged into the bathroom. Her hair was splayed like a fan, and her eyes— Her eyes were rose red.

Kelsey took care of her morning ablutions before going into Morgan's room. Her eyes took in the rumpled covers, the pillow on the floor and the Princess Tiana backpack, but the bed was empty. She frowned. Then rushed into Morgan's bathroom. She wasn't in there.

"Morgan!" she yelled, dragging back the shower curtain to look in the tub. Kelsey rushed back into her room and pulled back the blanket to see if she was underneath the covers. Nothing. She cocked her ears, her heart thumping. The house felt empty.

Telling herself not to panic, Kelsey called out again, "Morgan!" She skittered over to her nightstand and snatched up her phone. She called Zach as she raced down the stairs. "Morgan!" Kelsey ran through the kitchen and all the rooms on the main floor, but she didn't see her. "Morgan!" she screamed at the top of her lungs.

"Zach, have you seen Morgan?" she asked when he answered the phone. She tried to catch her breath. Her heart raced.

"Morgan?" he asked, sounding sleepy.

She looked at the clock and saw it was a little after six that morning.

"Yes. I can't find her," she breathed out. "Please tell me she's by you." She paced back and forth and her hands shook.

"No. I haven't seen her." He sounded more alert. "Let me go ask Mia. We went to bed pretty late last night." Kelsey could hear his footsteps and told herself to be calm. "I don't see her. Maybe she's downstairs." He called out for Mia, but his tone suggested he wasn't alarmed. That relaxed Kelsey. Somewhat.

"She's got to be there," Kelsey spat out, typing a text into her Three Divas group. "Please, God. Let her be."

9-1-1. Morgan's missing.

"Mia!" Zach called out. His voice now held urgency, and he was wide-awake. "Mia! Where could she be?"

"They've run off together," Kelsey said. "Oh, no. This is all my fault."

"I'm on my way over there," Zach said. "They couldn't have gone far. I'll call 9-1-1. Stay on the line."

"What if somebody snatched them? What if someone took our babies and we don't ever see them again?" Kelsey broke into tears and ran out her front door. "Morgan! Mia!" she yelled, running into her backyard. She searched the tree house, then the bushes, scratching her arms, but the girls weren't there.

Her phone rang. It was Jade, but she didn't answer because she was waiting for Zach to merge the call. When she heard the operator, Kelsey fell apart. Zach quickly told the operator that the girls were missing.

"Find them," she screamed. "Please find my girls."

She saw his truck coming toward her house and raced inside to put on her shoes. She was still wearing her nightdress, but Kelsey didn't care. Her body shook as she jumped into Zach's truck. He swerved out of the driveway and circled their neighborhood.

Sienna called next. This time she answered.

"Did you find her?"

"No. And Mia must be with her. Zach and I are driving around the block." She kept her eyes trained for the girls. "Do me a favor. Call Jade. Can you guys search the playground across from the development?"

"Got it." Sienna ended the call.

Zach and Kelsey searched the entire development, but they didn't see anything. He headed back to Kelsey's house. The cops had arrived. Several officers stood on her lawn, others were by the window and it looked like there were others heading into her backyard.

"Did you find them?" Kelsey bellowed.

"No, ma'am," the officer said in a grave tone once he had introduced himself. "Do you have a picture?"

"It's inside." She hadn't taken her purse with her.

Zach pulled out a picture of Mia from his wallet. "They're identical."

"When was the last time you saw them?"

She tried to think. To remember. "About ten. I put her into bed." She felt like she was going to pass out. Zach came over and held on to her.

"Do you know how they got out of the house?" Officer Helmsworth asked.

She placed a hand on her heaving chest. "I didn't see any broken windows. She must have gone through the front door."

"Was it unlocked?"

"I—I don't know." She swung a panicked gaze to Zach. "I rushed outside, but I don't remember unlocking the door."

A couple of officers went to knock on her neighbor's door. Her stomach clenched, and her legs buckled. All she could think was that the girls might be in danger. Zach's strong arms kept her from falling on the concrete.

She spotted Sienna's van, and she could see Jade sprinting toward her house.

"Do you know why they would want to leave?" the officer asked.

She covered her head with her hands. This was a nightmare. "I—I…" She couldn't confess it was all her fault. Kelsey leaned into Zach, welcoming his presence.

"They live in separate houses, and they want to be together," Zach supplied.

"I see."

"Kelsey!" Jade dashed closer, waving her hands. "I've found them. Mia and Morgan are at my house."

At those words, Kelsey could have cried. "What? Are they okay?"

"I was on my way here when I found them asleep in Izzy's old playhouse," Jade said, jogging up the driveway. "I didn't have the heart to wake them. Izzy is with them."

"I'm glad for good news," the cop said before backing off to summon his colleagues.

Kelsey fell to the ground, but this time her tears were caused by relief.

Zach pulled her to stand. "I'll go get them," he said, taking off toward Jade's house.

She fell into Sienna's and Jade's arms. "I'll never keep them away from each other again."

When Zach saw the girls snuggled with their arms about each other, his heart melted. Dropping to his knees, he gave God thanks for protecting his daughters. Yes, they were both his children, and he didn't know why it had taken something so dramatic to make him see that. To accept what his heart had been telling him all along.

Kelsey had been filled with self-recrimination, but in truth, he was the selfish one. If he hadn't refused to open his heart, the girls would have been together and they wouldn't have tried to run away. Thankfully, they had gone to Jade's house.

"Thank you for watching them," he said to Izzy before lifting both girls in his arms. Neither one awakened.

"I'm just glad they were here," Izzy said with tears in her eyes.

Kelsey rounded the corner with Sienna and Jade by her side. When she saw him, she raced over to where he stood and held out her arms.

"I've got them," Zach said. "I've got our girls. Let's go home." Then he led his family into his house. Zach took the girls upstairs into Mia's room and settled them on her bed. He stood in awe when even in sleep, they moved their bodies until they were inches apart. He felt a presence behind him and turned to see Kelsey standing by the door.

"Did you see that?" he whispered.

Her eyes welled. "Yes. Their love for each other is wonderful."

"So is my love for you," Zach said, holding out a hand.

She gasped. "What are you saying?" She lifted her hand before lowering it to her side.

He hated knowing that his actions—or rather, nonactions—made her insecure. There was only one way to remedy that. Zach placed his index finger over his lips and mouthed, "Let's talk outside."

She followed him into his kitchen and wrapped

her arms about herself. "I don't want you saying something you don't mean because the girls scared you this morning."

"I'm not. I'm a man, not a martyr," he said with a chuckle. Zach stepped into her personal space and chucked her under the chin. "Kelsey, I'm in love with you. When the girls were missing, my panic wasn't just for Mia. It was for you and Morgan as well. It made me realize that I was being foolish. I've been thinking that if I don't say the words, what I feel isn't real. My heart made room for you weeks ago, but I was too stubborn to admit it. My focus was on Sandy and how much I loved her. I did. But she's gone. What we had was wonderful, but she's not here, and she would have wanted me to be happy."

He cocked his head. "I hope I'm not too late. I hope you'll have me. And my love. Because I love you with everything I have to offer and all I will have to give. I want to spend the rest of my life loving you as you deserve. I saw you put your house up for sale, and I'm offering you the chance to live in mine—for a hefty price, of course."

She lifted a brow. "How much?"

He dropped to his knees and reached for her hands. "Your heart. Your love. You have to tell me every day that you love me. Kelsey Harris,

I never expected I would fall in love again. I thought if I loved, then it meant I would lose. But if I only have five minutes left in this world, I want all of those minutes to be spent with you—and our daughters. Mia needs a mom and Morgan needs a dad, and I'm ready to fill that vacancy. Are you?"

To his surprise, Kelsey also got on her knees.

"I don't think that's how it's traditionally done," he said.

"I know, but nothing about this is traditional. God gave me a daughter and then a husband. Wherever you are and on whatever level, I'm ready to meet you there. We're a team."

"I love you so much," he said, then took her left hand in his. "Will you marry me?"

"Yes, I'd be honored to be your wife and the mother for our daughters," Kelsey said. Her eyes shone as she cried.

He held up a hand and went into Mia's room and rifled through her hair accessories bin. Then he returned to Kelsey, slipped to his knees and slid the black rubber band on her ring finger. "I'll replace that. I promise." Zach cupped her head in the palm of his hand, tilted her head back and kissed her. This time, Zach snaked his arms around her waist and held nothing back. All the love he felt, Zach expressed without words. When he ended the kiss, he said, "We need a quick wedding and a long honeymoon."

She giggled and blushed. "I agree."

Together they stood.

"How does three weeks sound?" he asked.

"That's way too soon," she said, shaking her head. "This is my one and only marriage. I want a proper dress and to plan a decent reception."

"Get Sienna and Jade to help. I want to celebrate our union before the girls go back to school."

She tapped her chin. "Remember, we planned to take the girls to Disney World for their birthday. I say we do a quick weekend getaway for our honeymoon and spend time with the girls as a family."

He slapped his forehead. "Speaking of the girls, Frances never showed up yesterday."

Kelsey paused. "Yes, Morgan told me. I didn't ask her too much, because Morgan didn't seem upset about it. What do you think happened?"

"Mia told me she was glad Frankie didn't come. Trent reached out to her attorney. It turns out that Frankie was offered a gig in Switzerland. The meeting with the sponsors was on the same day and time as her meeting her daughters. She's dropping the custody case."

"Wow. I thought I would be rejoicing or doing backflips, but I feel sad for Frankie. I think she wants to be a mother but she's afraid of the responsibility." Her voice held sadness. "She's missing out on two special girls."

"I'm ecstatic this is over, but like you, I would want our daughters—I love saying that—to know the woman who chose to bring them here." He cleared his throat. "I reached out to Frankie and told her whenever she's ready, we're open to the girls being in her life. She hasn't responded yet, but I feel in time she will."

When Kelsey nodded, Zach's heart warmed. It felt good that they were in sync. She tapped her chin. "You know, people might think we're getting married just because of the girls. They might not believe this is a love match."

"People have gotten married for less. I don't care what they think," he said. "We know the truth. If the girls were taken from us tomorrow, I'd still marry you."

Her mouth dropped, and she brushed her index finger on the rubber band. "You would?"

"Yes," he said, without hesitation. "I want you, Kelsey. If you didn't come with a package and I didn't have a package, I would still want you. I would still be asking you to marry me."

She flung her arms around him and smiled. "And I would still say yes."

Chapter Twenty-Two

Large puzzle pieces lay scattered on Zach's rug. Zach had moved his coffee table out of the way so they all could build this special puzzle together. Sienna had suggested they get a picture of all four of them made into a large puzzle so they could put their family together before Kelsey and Zach shared the news of their engagement.

It had been the longest seven days while Kelsey waited for the package delivery. But she had used most of that time packing boxes. Her sister's home had sold after two days on the market. Kelsey had set the closing for a couple days before her wedding. She had already selected a venue on a country estate and had reserved separate rooms for her, Zach and their girls. Sienna and Jade were overseeing all the details for her and Zach's wedding, and Kelsey had been grateful for their help.

Her wedding.

Imagine that.

"Are you ready to work on this puzzle with us?"

"Yes," Morgan said. "I've never seen such a big puzzle piece." She cupped one in her hand.

Kelsey's excitement overflowed. "We're going to hang this puzzle on the wall when we're done, so I'm really glad for your help."

"I'm really good at puzzles," Mia said, holding two pieces up, with her tongue between her teeth.

Zach rubbed his hands together and winked at Kelsey. Her heart skipped a beat. Keeping this secret from the girls had been a major feat. She couldn't wait to see their faces. They began to put the puzzle together.

"I know what this is," Mia said when they were halfway complete. "This is us."

"Wow. This is cool," Morgan said.

Zach picked up a puzzle piece, and Kelsey picked up another. "Girls, Kelsey and I have some big news."

"We don't want to go with Frankie." Mia slung an arm around her sister's shoulder. "We're staying here."

Zach scooted close and tucked them under

his arms. "You don't have to worry about that anymore. Frankie wants you to stay with us." They clapped their hands and shouted with glee.

Once they had settled down, Zach held out a hand, and Kelsey tented hers with his. "We have something else to tell you."

Four eyes went wide, and two mouths dropped.

"Zach and I are getting married," Kelsey yelled out. The girls squealed and pounced on Zach and Kelsey with enough force that they fell back on the floor. A tickling match ensued, breaking apart the puzzle, but no one cared.

"We get to live together," the girls said.

"Are you going to have a wedding like *Beauty and the Beast*?" Mia asked.

"Yes," Kelsey said. "And we'd love for you to be our flower girls."

"Yay!" Morgan shouted. "This is the best day of my life." Both girls climbed in her lap, pressing tiny kisses on her face.

"Can we call you Mom?" Morgan asked, her eyes shining.

Kelsey nodded, swallowing the lump in her chest. She wiped her eyes. "I'd love nothing more."

"I get a new mommy," Mia yelled, kicking her feet.

"What about me?" Zach asked, sounding like he felt left out.

Morgan went over to him and slobbered his cheek with a raspberry. "You can be my daddy, too, if you want."

His eyes glossed. "It would be my honor."

Mia pumped her fists in the air. "We're going to be a family."

Kelsey held out her hands. "Family for life." They joined hands and finished putting their family together.

Two days before their wedding, disaster struck.

Kelsey and Zach had marveled before giving God praise.

There had been a sudden thunderstorm and a couple tornadoes. Two buildings in the town got touched, one minor, one major—Millennial House of Praise and Divine Realty. Millennial needed a few shingles replaced. *Divine Realty* had been smashed. Or as Mia and Morgan said, "Hulk smashed." Only rubble remained.

The rumor was Gerald had already skipped town. No one was sorry to see him leave.

But today, as Zach stood under the awning and awaited his bride, the sky was a clear, bright blue, and though the late-summer sun came with significant heat, they were grateful for a picturesque day.

August, his best man, stood next to him and teased, "I can't believe you're brave enough to do this again." Then he chuckled. "I'm just kidding, man. I'm glad you found love."

Zach adjusted his bow tie and elbowed his friend in the side. "Tag, you're it."

"No. No. Take that back," August said, sounding superstitious.

"You're a man of God," Zach laughed. "You know that's not how it works."

August pulled out his handkerchief and mopped his brow. "I know, but you can never be too careful."

Deacon Rose cleared his throat. "We're about to begin." He was licensed in Delaware to perform weddings, and he had been overjoyed when Zach asked him to officiate, even shedding a tear of happiness. Zach had been caught off guard by his display of love.

Scanning the crowd, Zach nodded to the boys from the juvenile center, who had been cleared to attend his wedding. Seeing them in their dress shirts and ties, Zach whispered a prayer for God to change the path for them. He searched for one person in particular, but Frankie hadn't shown.

The processional music began playing. Guests scrambled to their seats as the bridal party came forward. Izzy, Jade and Sienna walked down the aisle wearing wine-colored dresses. Then Mia and Morgan followed, throwing flowers on the floor, in the air, at the crowd. Zach cracked up at their antics.

Then his bride appeared, and he lost his breath.

Dressed in white, holding irises in her hand, Kelsey was a vision. She took a tentative step forward. Then another.

"Hurry up, Mommy," Mia shouted at the top of her lungs.

"Run, Mommy," Morgan yelled.

Zach tried to quiet them, but the crowd egged them on.

Kelsey bunched her dress in her hands and dashed down the aisle. It was certainly an untraditional entrance.

But for Kelsey, Zach, Mia and Morgan, it was perfect.

* * * * *

If you enjoyed this book, pick up these other sweet romances from Love Inspired.

Building Her Amish Dream
by Jo Ann Brown

Their Unpredictable Path
by Jocelyn McClay

The Veteran's Vow
by Jill Lynn

Secrets of Their Past
by Allie Pleiter

Fatherhood Lessons
by Gabrielle Meyer

*Find more great reads at
www.LoveInspired.com.*

Dear Reader,

I hope you enjoyed reading Kelsey and Zach's journey to love, my first book for the Love Inspired imprint. This story was inspired by the hit sitcom *Sister, Sister*. Being a twin myself—fraternal—I love reading about twins, and I love the bond they share. But there is something even more special when you have twins as matchmakers.

Though Zach battled grief and Kelsey struggled with doubt, they were each able to heal and find strength through God's Word, putting their hope in Him. Once they could do this, they found their happy-ever-after.

I would love to hear from you. Please connect with me on Facebook or visit my website to learn more about me at www.zoeymariejackson.com.

Blessings,
Zoey

Get 4 FREE REWARDS!

We'll send you 2 FREE Books plus 2 FREE Mystery Gifts.

FREE
Value Over
$20

Both the **Love Inspired®** and **Love Inspired® Suspense** series feature compelling novels filled with inspirational romance, faith, forgiveness, and hope.

YES! Please send me 2 FREE novels from the Love Inspired or Love Inspired Suspense series and my 2 FREE gifts (gifts are worth about $10 retail). After receiving them, if I don't wish to receive any more books, I can return the shipping statement marked "cancel." If I don't cancel, I will receive 6 brand-new Love Inspired Larger-Print books or Love Inspired Suspense Larger-Print books every month and be billed just $5.99 each in the U.S. or $6.24 each in Canada. That is a savings of at least 17% off the cover price. It's quite a bargain! Shipping and handling is just 50¢ per book in the U.S. and $1.25 per book in Canada.* I understand that accepting the 2 free books and gifts places me under no obligation to buy anything. I can always return a shipment and cancel at any time. The free books and gifts are mine to keep no matter what I decide.

Choose one: ☐ **Love Inspired**
Larger-Print
(122/322 IDN GNWC)

☐ **Love Inspired Suspense**
Larger-Print
(107/307 IDN GNWN)

Name (please print)

Address   Apt. #

City   State/Province   Zip/Postal Code

Email: Please check this box ☐ if you would like to receive newsletters and promotional emails from Harlequin Enterprises ULC and its affiliates. You can unsubscribe anytime.

Mail to the **Harlequin Reader Service:**
IN U.S.A.: P.O. Box 1341, Buffalo, NY 14240-8531
IN CANADA: P.O. Box 603, Fort Erie, Ontario L2A 5X3

Want to try 2 free books from another series? Call 1-800-873-8635 or visit www.ReaderService.com.

*Terms and prices subject to change without notice. Prices do not include sales taxes, which will be charged (if applicable) based on your state or country of residence. Canadian residents will be charged applicable taxes. Offer not valid in Quebec. This offer is limited to one order per household. Books received may not be as shown. Not valid for current subscribers to the Love Inspired or Love Inspired Suspense series. All orders subject to approval. Credit or debit balances in a customer's account(s) may be offset by any other outstanding balance owed by or to the customer. Please allow 4 to 6 weeks for delivery. Offer available while quantities last.

Your Privacy—Your information is being collected by Harlequin Enterprises ULC, operating as Harlequin Reader Service. For a complete summary of the information we collect, how we use this information and to whom it is disclosed, please visit our privacy notice located at corporate.harlequin.com/privacy-notice. From time to time we may also exchange your personal information with reputable third parties. If you wish to opt out of this sharing of your personal information, please visit readerservice.com/consumerschoice or call 1-800-873-8635. **Notice to California Residents**—Under California law, you have specific rights to control and access your data. For more information on these rights and how to exercise them, visit corporate.harlequin.com/california-privacy.

LIRLIS22

COUNTRY LEGACY COLLECTION

19 FREE BOOKS IN ALL!

Cowboys, adventure and romance await you in this new collection! Enjoy superb reading all year long with books by bestselling authors like Diana Palmer, Sasha Summers and Marie Ferrarella!

COMING NEXT MONTH FROM
Love Inspired

MISTAKEN FOR HIS AMISH BRIDE
North Country Amish • by Patricia Davids

Traveling to Maine to search for family, Mari Kemp is injured in an accident—and ends up with amnesia. Mistakenly believing she's the fiancée he's been corresponding with, Asher Fisher will do anything to help Mari recover her memories. But can she remember the past in time to see their future?

THE AMISH ANIMAL DOCTOR
by Patrice Lewis

Veterinarian Abigail Mast returns to her Amish community to care for her ailing mother and must pick between her career and the Amish life. Her handsome neighbor Benjamin Troyer isn't making the decision any easier. An impossible choice could lead to her greatest reward...

HER EASTER PRAYER
K-9 Companions • by Lee Tobin McClain

To heal from a past tragedy, Emily Carver and service dog Lady have devoted themselves to teaching children—including handyman Dev McCarthy's troubled son. But Dev's struggles with reading might need their help more. Can they learn to trust each other and write a happy ending to their story?

KEEPING THEM SAFE
Sundown Valley • by Linda Goodnight

Feeling honor bound to help others, rancher Bowie Trudeau is instantly drawn to former best friend Sage Walker—and her young niece and nephew—when she returns thirteen years later. Certain she'll leave again, Bowie's determined to not get attached. But this little family might just show him the true meaning of home...

A FOSTER MOTHER'S PROMISE
Kendrick Creek • by Ruth Logan Herne

Opening her heart and home to children in need is Carly Bradley's goal in life. But when she can't get through to a troubled little girl in her care, she turns to gruff new neighbor Mike Morris. Closed off after a tragic past, Mike might discover happiness next door...

AN ALASKAN SECRET
Home to Hearts Bay • by Heidi McCahan

Wildlife biologist Asher Hale never expected returning home to Hearts Bay, Alaska, would put him face-to-face with his ex Tess Madden—or that she would be his son's second-grade teacher. Their love starts to rekindle, but as buried memories come to light, could their second chance be ruined forever?

LOOK FOR THESE AND OTHER LOVE INSPIRED BOOKS WHEREVER BOOKS ARE SOLD, INCLUDING MOST BOOKSTORES, SUPERMARKETS, DISCOUNT STORES AND DRUGSTORES.

LICNM0222